EB
JP
WWW

DISCARDED

SILVERSTRAND

Working for the Distress Call Agency, Tara Dereham travels from London to the seaside town of Silverstrand, to help Mrs Ward run her guesthouse. But when Mrs Ward falls ill, Tara has to manage the business and care for her client's grandson, helped by one of the guests, Steven Harris. But there is a secret in the Ward family, and danger looms for Tara as she learns more of the secret and of the people concerned.

Books by Diney Delancey
in the Linford Romance Library:

FOR LOVE OF OLIVER
AN OLD-FASHIONED LOVE
LOVE'S DAWNING

DINEY DELANCEY

SILVERSTRAND

Complete and Unabridged

LINFORD
Leicester

First published in Great Britain in 1983 by
Robert Hale Limited
London

First Linford Edition
published 2006
by arrangement with
Robert Hale Limited
London

British Library CIP Data

Delancey, Diney
Silverstrand.—Large print ed.—
Linford romance library
1. Love stories
2. Large type books
I. Title
823.9'14 [F]

ISBN 1–84617–528–3

Published by
F. A. Thorpe (Publishing)
Anstey, Leicestershire

Set by Words & Graphics Ltd.
Anstey, Leicestershire
Printed and bound in Great Britain by
T. J. International Ltd., Padstow, Cornwall

This book is printed on acid-free paper

1

'I need someone straight away,' said Mrs Ward. 'I'm entirely without help. The agency said you would be available at once.' Her voice was strained and she sounded desperate.

'I can come straight away, don't worry,' soothed Tara, who had been out on such emergency calls before. 'I've only to collect the file from the office and I'll be with you by late afternoon, early evening.'

There were, however, several delays at the office and it was already early evening when Tara turned off the main road and followed the sign to Silverstrand. She had never been there before and as always when tackling a new assignment she felt excitement stir within her. What would it be like? Each job was unique and it was this variety in her work which pleased Tara and added an element of challenge; her life had never been humdrum or boring since she had signed on with the Distress Call Agency. Though many of the jobs she had undertaken were in London, allowing her to work from her own flat, there had also been occasional assignments, like this one, which took her away for days, or even weeks, at a time and so offered her the extra interest of seeing new places and meeting new people.

She drove into Silverstrand and discovered a typical small resort town with a promenade, skateboarders' paradise, stretching smooth and grey along the front above the beach; a pier jutting resolutely into the sea and all solemnly regarded by tall grey stone houses, three and four storeys high, whose tall windows on the first floor opened to tiny iron-guarded balconies. Coloured swimsuits dangling from window catches belied their austerity and bed and breakfast signs abounded. Below the promenade which appeared to reach the length of the town was a wide sweep of sand curving away towards a distant headland. Almost deserted, gleaming in the evening sun as the last few families headed for their hotels and boarding houses, it was the stretch of silvery sand from which the town took its name.

The promenade was not deserted however, on the contrary it was alive with strolling couples and lounging groups of youngsters, waiting for the evening to begin. Tara stopped the car at an information kiosk to ask her way. The man there was just closing for the day rolling down the shutters and locking the door.

'Old Court Guest House? Not far, dear; down towards the end of the prom, turn right into the High Street and you'll find Grove Road down there on your left. Old Court is along on the left hand side.'

Tara thanked him and following his instructions soon drew up at her destination, Old Court Guest House. It had been converted from two of a row of houses, huge, built in grey stone like so many along the sea front. Its rather austere facade was enlivened by white-painted window boxes from which petunias tumbled in profusion, purple, pink and white glowing against the rough grey stone surrounding them. The neat front garden was sheltered by a low stone wall topped with railings and in front of the second half of the hotel there was a tarmacked area where guests could park their cars. 'Old Court' was painted in gold on the fan light above the front door and a card saying 'No Vacancies' was propped up in the window beside it.

Tara parked the car and taking her suitcase from the boot approached the half-open front door and rang the bell. A harassed-looking woman came to answer and Tara's immediate impression of her was greyness. Her grizzled hair hung limp and lank about her tired, pallid face and she was dressed in a shapeless grey frock which dropped across her bosom and sagged at the hemline. She was a picture of depression and exhaustion. When she saw Tara standing on the step, suitcase in hand, she said, 'I'm sorry we've no room. Can't you see the sign?'

'Mrs Ward?' said Tara, setting down her case and extending her hand. 'I'm Tara Dereham, we spoke on the phone earlier today.' Mrs Ward passed a hand wearily across her forehead to push back an errant lock of hair, before shaking Tara's hand and saying, 'I'm sorry, Miss Dereham, I didn't realise it was you. Please come in.' She led the way indoors, passing through the narrow hallway into a large kitchen at the back of the house. Crockery, pots and pans were stacked on every available surface, oddments of food littered the table and above the clutter sheets hung from an airer suspended from the ceiling. Mrs Ward unceremoniously tipped a large cat off one chair and indicating another to Tara, sank down with her arms on the table.

'I'm sorry about the mess. I've just

served the evening meal, and everyone was in tonight. Typical on a night when I've no help at all.' She looked tired, old and defeated and Tara felt a wave of sympathy.

'Don't worry about it,' she said. 'That's what I'm here for, isn't it? Now if you'll just show me my room, I can change and then I'll get this lot cleaned up.'

Mrs Ward stared at her for a moment before relief swept across her face and she managed a weak smile.

'Would you? Would you really start at once? That would be marvellous, then I can give some time to Paul, read him a story before he settles down.' With new vitality she got to her feet and led Tara upstairs. The bedroom she showed her was at the back of the house on the first floor. It was small but neat and clean. The half-opened sash window had its window box on the wide outside sill and looked out over a small paved courtyard surrounded by ivy-covered stone walls, one with an old door set into it. The evening sun cast shadows across the courtyard but one corner was still bathed in gold and there, sitting on a garden seat, his knees tucked up beneath him, was a small boy, aged about six, looking at a book.

Mrs Ward glanced down at him. 'That's Paul, my grandson,' she said with a smile, 'my daughter's son.' She turned back to Tara and said briskly, 'I'll get him off to bed if you'll really tackle the kitchen.'

Two hours later Tara sat at the kitchen table with a plate of cold meat and salad in front of her and a cup of coffee at her elbow. The kitchen was immaculate now, everything washed up and tidied away. The tables in the dining room were laid up for breakfast and the sheets folded and piled neatly into the linen cupboard on the top landing.

'You're fantastic,' said Mrs Ward as she dropped into a chair opposite. 'It was all getting out of hand. I had a girl living in but her mother was taken ill and she had to go home immediately. I thought it would only be for a few days, but after a fortnight she phoned to say she wouldn't be back. So all the help I have now is old Mrs Vernon who comes in to help clean for a couple of hours each day. Everything had piled up on me here. It's very hard work in the season even with full-time help, but I just couldn't cope another day on my own, and of course everyone's looking for staff this time of year.' She chatted on as Tara ate her supper, finding relief in pouring out her troubles to a sympathetic ear.

'We're not full up as a matter of fact,' said Mrs Ward. 'I just put up the 'No Vacancies' sign because I was run off my feet looking after the guests we have got. We offer full board you know, and most of them take advantage of it. Well, it's no distance from the beach, worth coming back for lunch, particularly if the weather's not fine enough to picnic. Now you've come I'll take the sign down again, our season's not a very long one so we have to make the most of it.' She pushed the fruit bowl towards Tara who selected an orange, then sitting back to peel it said, 'Well, the best thing is for you to tell me exactly what you want me to do for you, and how I can be of the most help.'

Mrs Ward smiled across at her, and noticed fleetingly what an attractive girl Tara Dereham was. Her auburn hair was long and thick, and at the moment tied back from her face, knotted at her neck with an emerald scarf. Her eyes, a translucent green, were set wide apart and returned Mrs Ward's gaze expectantly. She was not the sort of girl Mrs Ward normally employed, a youngster fresh from school, or down from university on vacation. Tara was older, maybe twenty-five or six, and she had the confident air of someone used to looking after herself, and coping with the unexpected, calm and unflappable.

Suddenly aware that she had been staring, Mrs Ward said 'What? Oh, of course. Well, we serve breakfast between eight and nine. Then it's beds and bathrooms and general chores. Lunch is usually cold, I serve it buffet-style in the dining room, perhaps with soup to start and fruit or cheese to finish. You can have each afternoon off and be back to serve dinner between seven and eight. I'll do the cooking, though you can help prepare. Once it's cleared and the breakfast tables are set you're free for the evening.'

Tara nodded. 'That sounds straight-forward enough.'

Mrs Ward sighed. 'I wish it was,' she said. 'There's Paul, too, to be consid-ered. He's very good but he's very much on his own. I can't give him nearly enough time. He's such a quiet little boy, he needs more attention, needs drawing out.'

Paul was obviously one of Mrs Ward's greatest worries and once talking of him she found it hard to stop. 'The trouble is I'm the wrong generat-ion,' she said. 'He needs someone younger than an ageing grandmother, but,' she let out a sigh, 'we're all the family each other has got, so I have to do the best I can.'

'His parents?' asked Tara, tentatively.

Mrs Ward's confiding manner disappeared and she answered stiffly, 'I don't want to discuss them.'

Tara's response to Mrs Ward's abrupt change of tone was cool politeness, and she said, 'Believe me, Mrs Ward, I am not trying to pry into your private affairs, but if there is something unusual about Paul's background it would surely be better that I knew so that I can avoid causing any awkwardness or embarrassment with an unfortunate remark or comment.'

Mrs Ward relaxed a little and said, 'Of course you're right. I'm sorry, I didn't mean to snap. It was all so terrible that we are doing our best to forget it. Put everything behind us. That's why we moved here, away from everyone who would know us or recognise us. We had to start again, so, to provide a home and an income I took on this place.' She paused and Tara waited, reluctant to ask what it was that had caused them to need a fresh start, yet intrigued to know.

Mrs Ward looked across the table at her and said, 'What I'm telling you now is in the strictest confidence, Miss Dereham.'

'Tara,' put in Tara gently.

'Tara, then. No one here knows what happened. If anyone has asked I've said that Paul is an orphan. I could say the same to you, I suppose, but somehow I want to tell you the truth. I've no friends down here, nobody to confide in, and they say it's easier to talk to a stranger. Perhaps it really is.' Again she paused and then taking a deep breath as if to strengthen her resolve she said, 'His mother, my daughter Jane, is dead; she was murdered.'

Tara saw tears filling the old lady's eyes.

'And his father?' she asked gently.

'His father. He was the one who killed her. He killed her, my Jane.'

Tara stared. 'He murdered his wife?' she said incredulously.

'Oh, he had a clever lawyer. He got away with manslaughter.' Mrs Ward spoke bitterly. 'He's in prison now, but not for much longer. Then he'll try to find us.'

'Does he know where you are?'

'No. We moved right away. I told no one where we were going. Paul uses my name now.'

'Does he know?' asked Tara. 'Paul, I mean. Does he know what happened?'

'No, I don't think so. He was only two at the time; he remembers nothing.'

'But what does he think about his parents?'

'I've told him his mother was killed in a car crash, and that his father went away. I told him his father didn't love him and didn't want him and that we were happier without him. Paul agrees.'

'You turned Paul against him?'

'Wouldn't you? The man who'd murdered his mother? Just suppose he does manage to find us, am I supposed to hand over my daughter's son to her murderer? Paul's mine now and Simon Hamilton won't get his hands on him ever if I can possibly stop him. I'll fight him through every court in the land.' Angry colour had flooded Mrs Ward's pale cheeks, high spots of red blotching her face, and the handkerchief she had taken out to dab her eyes was twisted viciously between her fingers.

'We've got to watch Paul,' she said tensely. 'I wouldn't put it past that man to try to kidnap him. I don't let him out alone now; his father must be due out sometime soon.'

'Won't the prison let you know when?' asked Tara.

'They might, if they knew where we were.'

'Don't they know?'

'The only person who knows is my solicitor, Andrew Harper. He was a great friend of Jane's and a tower of strength to me throughout the trial. He's asked the prison to let him know when Simon's due out, saying he's acting for us, but he refused them our address so they may not let him know; he's not a relative or anything.' Mrs Ward slumped back into her chair and Tara could see why the old lady had needed help so urgently; she was almost at breaking point, worries about running the guest house single-handed crowding in and piling upon the permanent fear she had for her grandson, and the increasing terror she had of his father.

'I'm glad you told me,' said Tara, but she spoke with a calmness she did not feel. Inside, her mind was whirling; what on earth had she become involved in? 'Don't worry. Between us we can take care of Paul, and keep watching out for his father. I've no friends in this area, so in my free time during the afternoon I'll take Paul about a bit if you like. Surely there's no need to keep him inside all the time? His father won't easily recognise him now anyway, will he? I mean, four years is a long time and Paul's changed from a toddler into a strong young boy. If this Simon Hamilton doesn't turn up in the next few weeks, he probably never will; you can't spend the rest of your life, or Paul's, with one eye over your shoulder in case he does, you know.'

'No,' agreed Mrs Ward, 'I can't. But I expect I will,' she added with a sigh. And Tara, going over the conversation in her head later as she drifted into sleep, knew that Mrs Ward was right; the threat from Simon Hamilton would always be there, a shadow at her shoulder.

2

The next few days were so busy that Tara had little time to brood on the possible arrival of a murderer on the scene. Every moment of the morning from seven o'clock on was devoted to the running of the guest house. Old Court was not yet full; there was still one room free, the one that paired with Tara's across the landing, but the guests that were in residence were fairly demanding, all taking the full board option so that Tara was seldom free before three o'clock. Even then her time was not entirely her own as Mrs Ward succeeded in suppressing her fears a little and allowed Tara to take Paul with her as she wandered round the town or explored the surrounding countryside in her car.

Tara felt drawn to the child at once. He was a solitary little boy and seemed to have no friends of his own; but once she had talked with him a while and offered to take him out he had slipped a confiding hand into hers and said, 'I could show you the beach if you like.' Tara accepted his offer with enthusiasm and they set off on the first of many expeditions together, slipping through the old door in the courtyard wall into the alley which led between high garden walls out to the end of the promenade. On reaching the end Tara turned towards the town, but Paul tugged her sleeve and said, 'No, not with the grockles, this way.'

'Grockles?' laughed Tara.

'The holiday people,' explained Paul. 'Come on, this way.'

He led her away from the crowded prom and busy sands along the road leading out of the town, then cutting down another track brought them to the sand dunes, topped with stiff dry grasses rustling and singing in the wind. Paul paused a moment to take off his shoes and then ran through the dry sand up the slopes of one sandhill, tumbling down into the softness of the sandy valley between it and the next. Laughing, he rolled in the sand, and Tara, infected by his sudden exuberance also removed her shoes and slipped and slithered down through the sand after him. Darting through the dunes as if a path led him onward, Paul took Tara to the highest point and from there pointed out the mouth of a river which emerged beside the headland. Still running they crossed the flat wet sand left by the receding tide until they reached the sluggish flow of water, brown across the sand, which was the river.

'This is where I like to come,' Paul said shyly. 'This is where the boats are. I like boats.'

Tara looked up the river. Sheltered in its curve and backed by the dunes she saw several boats rocking at moorings and a fleet of dinghies drawn up on a spit of sand above the high water mark. The place seemed deserted except for the seabirds which stalked the mudflat exposed by the ebbing tide, and its very solitude appealed to her. They stood in silence for a moment before she said, 'I can see why you come here, Paul, it's a lovely place, but isn't it a bit lonely?'

The boy shook his head. 'Often it's very busy. There's a yacht club and at weekends they race from here, and sometimes yachts cruising round the coast come in overnight or stay for a few days. But I like it best when there's no one. I'm going to have my own boat one day, but Gran says not yet; there's no one to teach me. You have to be ten before the yacht club'll help.'

'Well, that won't be long,' said Tara encouragingly.

'Four years,' answered Paul. 'Four years. It's a long time. It's ages.'

They walked up the river a little way and then cut back across the meadows to the dunes. Paul said very little and then he suddenly asked, 'Are you going to stay with us long, Tara?'

'I don't know,' she replied. 'Your

grandmother is still trying to get help locally. I work for an agency, you see, a sort of helping out agency, who send someone in an emergency. Once your grandmother has found other help I'll go back to London and be given another assignment.'

'What's an assignment?' enquired Paul with interest.

'A job. I've had some peculiar ones I can tell you.'

'Like what?' Paul's face showed an eagerness Tara had not seen before, so she recalled some of her more bizarre jobs for him.

'Well, one time I had to show an Arab prince of about eleven round London before he went off to his new school; and another I had to go to a castle in Scotland for a week to help in a ghost-hunt.'

Paul's eyes grew like saucers. 'Tell me about that.'

So Tara told him, embroidering the tale as she went along, and was still telling him about it when they reached the footpath through to Old Court's yard.

After that, every afternoon they went out together, visiting places of interest which Tara always enjoyed, exploring the country or sometimes simply scrambling over the hills which swept up from the sea until their hearts were pounding and their cheeks were flushed. In the evenings Paul played with his grandmother while Tara cleaned up the kitchen after they had served dinner. The days were long and when they were over Tara was quite happy to go upstairs and sit in the warm quietness of her room, the sash thrown open and the perfume of the evening drifting in. Sometimes she read, but often too tired to enjoy her book she sat looking down into the courtyard watching the colours fade to twilight and the twilight turn to night.

It was on an evening such as this about a week later that Tara had returned to her room to recover from a particularly gruelling day when the silent peace was shattered by a tremendous crash from somewhere below; a clatter which echoed into the darkness and set Tara's heart pounding. She leapt to her feet and leaned for a moment from her open window. A shaft of light from the uncurtained kitchen pierced the gloom but revealed nothing. The crash was followed by a deafening silence and pulling herself together sharply, Tara hastened out on to the landing and down the stairs to investigate. No one else appeared; the television blared behind the closed door of the television lounge, its viewers undisturbed. No other doors opened, not even Paul's on the top floor and so Tara was alone when she found Mrs Ward on the kitchen floor surrounded by broken crockery and glasses which she had been carrying on a tray.

At first Tara thought the old lady was dead and a cold sweat broke out on her forehead. She spun round, looking wildly in all directions as if to discover an intruder lurking in the shadowy hall, but immediately common sense came to her aid and she crossed the kitchen to where Mrs Ward was sprawled. Tara looked at the deathly pale face and the frail body limp as a discarded rag doll and knelt down beside her. She lifted one of Mrs Ward's hands and felt for a pulse. It was there, just, no more than a flutter beneath Tara's fingers; but Mrs Ward showed no other sign of life. Tara put down the old lady's hand, crossed to the telephone on the kitchen wall and dialled 999.

The ambulance arrived within minutes and carried the still unconscious Mrs Ward swiftly to the general hospital.

'You want to come along, love?' asked one of the ambulance men. 'Can if you like.'

'No, thank you,' said Tara, 'there's a little boy asleep upstairs. I'm responsible for him now, this is his grandmother.'

'Right you are,' said the man closing the ambulance door on Mrs Ward and the other ambulance man, 'Give the hospital a ring in a while and they'll tell you how she's going on. Looks like a stroke to me.'

They roared off into the night, klaxon blaring and Tara turned back into Old Court, to face the fact that she had to try and run the place single-handed, and at the same time cope with Paul. It was a daunting proposition and as she considered it Tara knew why Mrs Ward had called in the Distress Call Agency.

After the drama of the evening, Old Court seemed strangely normal; the only sign of anything untoward was the shattered china on the kitchen floor. Mechanically Tara began to clear it up while her brain decided what she should do. As soon as the floor was cleared she rang the hospital. It was too soon. They could tell her nothing except that Mrs Ward had been admitted and was in intensive care. They suggested that she call again in the morning. She boiled the kettle for a much needed coffee, wishing there was something stronger, but Old Court had no licence and she had never seen alcoholic drink of any kind there. Just then she heard Paul calling and hurried upstairs, mug of coffee in hand to see what he wanted.

'Gran, Gran.' The voice was shrill and frightened, and Tara pushed open the bedroom door to let the light flood in.

'Gran?'

'It's me, Tara. What's the matter, Paul?'

'Where's Gran? I want Gran. I've had a bad dream.'

Tara saw that the boy was sweating and she dropped on to the edge of his bed and smoothed his hair off his forehead.

'Never mind, Paul, you're awake now. It's all right now. Look, there's nothing here to be afraid of. You're boiling hot — let's take a blanket off your bed. That's probably why you had a nightmare, you know, because you were too hot.' Paul relaxed a little and his face lost the white fear which had glazed it when Tara first opened the door.

'Yes. Yes, I am a bit hot. Where's Gran?'

Tara had not intended to break the news of his grandmother's stroke until the morning but his persistent question needed an answer, so she decided she must give a truthful one. She took his hands in hers and said gently, 'I'm afraid she isn't very well, Paul. She's had to go into hospital so that she can get better.'

The fear returned to Paul's face and he said, 'What's the matter with her? Is she going to die?'

'They don't know what's the matter yet, but I don't think she's going to die. She's had to work very hard lately and she's probably just worn out. They'll be able to tell us more in the morning.'

Tara wanted to reassure the child, to give him the comfort he was grasping for and say that his grandmother was sure to get well, but Tara knew that the old lady was dangerously ill and dared not build Paul's hopes only to shatter them with worse news in the morning.

Paul stared at her, or through her; his eyes did not seem to register what they could see.

'I don't want Gran to die,' he said. 'I don't want her to die.'

Tara gathered him into her arms and whispered, 'They'll do all they can to make her well. The doctors are very clever, you know.'

'They didn't save my mummy.' Paul spoke loudly and bitterly. 'My mummy died. My daddy killed her, and when the doctor came to see they took her away. They took my daddy away, too. I hate him. He killed my mummy.'

Tara held the child away from her in horror and stared at the hatred in his pinched face. Paul was not supposed to know about his parents. Mrs Ward had told him his mother had been killed in a car crash; that his father had left and that he was virtually an orphan.

'Paul!' Tara exclaimed. 'Paul, that's a dreadful thing to say. Who told you such a dreadful thing?'

'Uncle Andrew. He told me last time

he came. He told me because he said I was old enough to know, that a man should know what has happened in his life.'

'But you're not a man!' cried Tara, appalled.

'I'm nearly seven,' said Paul indignantly, 'I don't want stories told to me. I was going to tell Gran not to pretend any more but Uncle Andrew said not to let her know I knew. He's coming out of prison soon, my father, and if he comes here I shall spit in his face and tell him to go away.' His brittle defiance snapped and he sobbed on Tara's shoulder. 'I don't want Gran to die. I don't want Gran to die. He might take me away and murder me.'

'He won't, I promise you he won't,' soothed Tara. 'If he comes here we'll call the police.'

'Are you going to stay? You won't leave, will you?' pleaded the child, looking up into Tara's face with wide frightened eyes.

'I won't leave, certainly not until we

have some idea of how your grandmother is. Now, who's this Uncle Andrew?'

'He's a man who comes down from London to see Gran sometimes. He always brings me something, and we talk about things.' Paul's voice was steadier now that he knew Tara was going to stay.

Very unsuitable things, too, thought Tara severely, but left the comment unmade as she felt the boy relax a little in her arms.

'Well, your grandmother did mention a solicitor one time, but I can't remember his name. Do you know his surname?'

The boy shook his head.

'Well, I'll try and find out in the morning and we'll contact him. Now, you must try to go back to sleep; I'll need your help tomorrow. We'll have a lot of work to do if we're to keep this place running. Will you help?'

Paul nodded vigorously. 'And I'll make Gran a 'Get Well' card.'

'Good idea,' agreed Tara, as she tucked him in once more. 'I'll leave the landing light on, then if you want me in the night you can find me easily. Night night, sleep well.'

Paul said goodnight and Tara went back down to the kitchen to telephone the Distress Call Agency on its twenty-four hour number so that they would know what had happened; they could give her advice and, if necessary, assistance. It almost certainly would be necessary, Tara decided as she lay in bed trying to sleep. Things at Old Court were more complicated than she had realised and she was still churning them round in her brain when she finally dropped into an uneasy sleep.

3

Tara woke early next morning and lay for a moment letting the events of the previous evening wash back into her mind, then with a sigh she climbed out of bed to start work on the breakfasts. She was just finishing the washing up when the phone rang. It was the office, returning her call.

'We aren't authorised to send you anyone else,' said Derek, her boss. 'The client has only contracted for you.'

'Well, I can't run this place on my own,' snapped Tara. 'What do you suggest?'

'In the circumstances I should try and engage help locally. You can get the client's authorisation for further help from us if she is able to give it of course. Otherwise you'll have to do the best you can.'

'Thank you very much,' snorted Tara

as she hung up. 'Get help locally,' she muttered. 'If Mrs Ward could have done that I wouldn't be here.' With a sigh she picked up the receiver and dialled the hospital. There was no change in Mrs Ward's condition. She was still in intensive care and not allowed visitors.

Mrs Vernon arrived and clattered round the kitchen collecting duster and broom. Tara explained about Mrs Ward and then on impulse said, 'You don't happen to know the name of Mrs Ward's solicitor do you? Andrew someone?'

''Er solicitor? No, Miss Tara, I wouldn't know that. Why?'

'Well, I felt I should get in touch with somebody about Mrs Ward being in hospital and Paul being left on his own. I'll just have to wait until they let me speak to her, I suppose.'

'Sorry, dear, I can't help. I'll do the dining room first, shall I? Let you get them beds made in peace.'

Paul came into the kitchen with a packet of felt pens and a sheet of paper.

'I'm going to do Gran's card now,' he announced, and settled himself at the kitchen table.

'Right, Paul. Good idea. I'm just going upstairs to do the beds and when I've done that we'll have some elevenses.'

She had almost finished upstairs when she heard the doorbell and then Paul calling to her.

'Tara! Tara! There's a man here wants to see you.'

'Coming,' called Tara and rather dishevelled, carrying the vacuum cleaner under one arm, she hurried downstairs.

Paul was still talking to the newcomer. 'Gran's not here, she's ill in hospital, so there's only Tara and me. Here's Tara now. She knows about guests.'

The man stood in a shaft of sunlight which flooded through the open front door. He greeted Tara with a smile, a smile that lit his entire face and was impossible not to return. His eyes, deepset and candid regarded her easily and his voice when he spoke was soft and deep.

'Good morning,' he said. 'I see you have a vacancies sign and wondered if you could accommodate me for a few days.' He gestured to the suitcase at his feet and went on, 'A week perhaps, possibly more?'

Tara had decided to remove the vacancies sign from the window as she had quite enough to cope with, without new guests but as she opened her mouth to express her regrets she heard herself saying, 'Of course. You're lucky, we have the one room left, if you'd care to see it.'

'Thank you.'

Tara led the way upstairs and the man followed carrying his suitcase. She threw open the door to the room opposite her own and showed him in.

'This will do very well,' he said.

'Fine,' said Tara and discovering that she was still smiling broadly, became more serious and said, 'If you'd care to come down and register Mr er . . . ?'

'Harris. Steven Harris.'

'Mr Harris. Paul will show you where the bathroom and dining room are, won't you, Paul?'

Paul, who had followed them upstairs, nodded vigorously and remarked, 'I'm helping Tara today 'cos Gran's ill. We're running the place on our own,' he added loftily.

Steven Harris smiled again. 'Are you indeed? Well done, Paul.'

Tara left Paul to show the new guest round and went down to the kitchen and then, realising she had not asked Steven Harris if he wanted full board, she climbed the stairs again to ask. As she came to the landing she heard Paul saying, 'She's gone to hospital, but Tara says she'll be better soon.'

'Is Tara your big sister?' asked Steven.

'No!' Paul laughed at the idea. 'Tara's our distress lady.'

'Sounds fascinating!' remarked Steven, but before he could ask any more questions Tara made her presence known.

The day passed far more easily than

Tara had imagined. Only four guests were in to lunch and so she and Paul were able to go out for a while in the afternoon.

'Can we go to the boatyard?' cried Paul as they set off. 'We could go and look at the lifeboat.'

Tara laughed and agreed. They set off along the beach and cut through the dunes to the river. They waved to Tom Gurney, the ferryman and he puttered across to fetch them in the little open ferry boat.

They spent a lovely afternoon poking round amongst the boats and looking at the lifeboat and when Tom Gurney dropped them back on their own side of the river a couple of hours later Paul was chattering excitedly about all he had seen and seemed to have forgotten his fear for his grandmother. However, when they got home he saw his card lying on the kitchen dresser.

'Oh, Tara, I never posted my card to Gran!' he cried in dismay. 'Can we go and do it now?'

'Paul, I can't go out again. I've got to cook the dinner. We haven't any stamps anyway. We'll have to do it tomorrow.'

'I want to go now!' scowled Paul. 'I can buy a stamp at the post office. It'll still be open. I've got some money in my money box if you can get it down for me.' He pointed to a pink elephant money box standing on the mantelpiece.

'All right,' agreed Tara reluctantly and reached the elephant down, 'but come straight back.'

Paul's scowl vanished, he took some money from his box and darted out of the house clutching it and his card. Tara watched him for a moment, smiling to see him swinging round each of the trees which lined the avenue, and then turned back to the chicken.

It was half an hour later as she closed the oven door on her cooking that she realised Paul had not yet returned. With Mrs Ward's fears echoing in her own head she hurried to the gate and looked down the road. It was deserted. Quickly she ran along to the corner where the road joined the High Street. The early evening promenaders were out and the High Street shops, all eager to make the most of a short season, still had their doors wide to the public. There was no sign of Paul coming back home and so she thrust her way through the crowds until she came to the main Post Office. Not ruled by the holidaymakers it was already closed. Desperate now, with her imagination working overtime, Tara began to call his name.

'Paul, Paul! Where are you, Paul?' A few heads turned, mildly interested, but children lost in the crowd were commonplace in Silverstrand and nobody offered Tara any assistance until a grey-haired man paused to say, ''E's prob'ly gorn 'ome, luv.'

Tara sighed and said 'Thank you, yes you're probably right.' Certainly it was no use standing in the high street calling his name so Tara turned her steps back to Old Court. As she opened the front door she called again but there was no answering call. Steven Harris appeared on the stairs and Tara said hopefully, 'You haven't seen Paul, have you Mr Harris?' Steven shook his head.

'Have you lost him?'

Tara explained and Steven replied, 'I shouldn't worry. He's probably stopped to look at something on the way home. Would you like me to go and have a look for him?'

Tara gave him a look of immense gratitude. 'Would you? I must get on with the dinner, and as he's not mine I feel extra responsible for Paul. Especially as . . . ' she stopped.

'Especially as?' prompted Steven.

'Nothing, really. His grandmother doesn't let him out on his own, and I did.'

'Don't worry, Tara' said Steven cheerfully. 'I'll find him.'

Still with fear nagging at her mind Tara turned her attention to the dinner, and it was with unbelievable relief that she heard Paul's piping voice in the hallway several minutes later.

'The wanderer returns,' announced Steven and pushed Paul gently in through the kitchen door.

'Paul. Thank God!' cried Tara gathering the surprised child to her. 'Where on earth have you been? You naughty boy!'

Paul struggled free of her arms and said, 'Only on the front. I met David Castle from school and we went to see the model boats. I'm all right.'

'I can see that,' said Tara, 'but I told you to come straight back.' Paul scowled at her tone and she sent him to wash his hands before he had his supper.

'Thank you very much for finding him,' said Tara to Steven as he, too, turned to leave the kitchen. Steven smiled and Tara found herself smiling again though a moment earlier her face had been grim with worry.

'No trouble,' he said and went upstairs.

Paul's fears for his grandmother

came flooding back as bedtime drew near and Tara had to spend some time calming him down so that he would sleep.

'Will you sleep in Gran's room so you're next door to me?' Paul asked, his lip trembling.

'Yes, all right,' Tara agreed, anxious to get the boy settled so she could clear up downstairs.

'I'll sleep in there. I won't be up for a little while yet though, so you go to sleep and I'll come and tuck you in again when I go to bed.'

Eventually Tara was able to leave Paul's room and return to the kitchen where the guests' dinner things were piled for washing up. As she saw it all waiting for her, Tara knew how Mrs Ward had felt the night she had arrived, but determined at least to do as well as the old lady had, Tara turned to and stacked the dishwasher.

'Would you like a hand?'

Steven's deep voice cut through her thoughts, making her start. She spun round. 'I'm sorry?'

'You look as if you could do with a hand,' he said, and without further comment he started work on the saucepans in the sink.

'You don't have to do that!' she exclaimed as he scoured a pan with an expert touch.

'I know. But from what the boy was telling me on the way back from the boating pool you're running this place entirely single-handed. You look pretty tired anyway.'

'I am a bit,' admitted Tara, 'if you're sure you don't mind.'

'Not a bit, I'm an expert,' Steven assured her, 'and afterwards you can put your feet up and recover with a large whisky, or gin or whatever.'

Together they reduced the chaos in the kitchen to some sort of order, and laid up the breakfast tables. Tara decided she must be thinking of Steven in the same sort of light as Mrs Ward had thought of her that first night and she giggled at the idea.

'Private joke?' enquired Steven.

'No, not really,' and Tara told him how she came to be at Old Court at all.

'And then this Mrs Ward upped and collapsed on you and left you holding the baby!'

Tara laughed at the way he expressed it but agreed that that was precisely what had happened.

'Two babies actually,' she added, sinking into Mrs Ward's armchair in the kitchen, 'the guest house which is her living and her home, and Paul who is her life.'

'No parents?' asked Steven, easing himself into a chair across the table from her. Tara was immediately on her guard. She realised she would have to give some explanation yet was bound not to reveal the truth about Paul's past, so she decided to stick to the story Mrs Ward had already allowed to circulate.

'Poor kid,' remarked Steven. 'No wonder he's scared of losing his grandmother as well; I'm not surprised you were worried when he disappeared this evening.'

Tara looked across at Steven, and liked what she saw; he had a strong face — not unlined, as if he'd known sorrow, but calm as if he had come to terms with it. Laughter lines were there, too, and his lightest smile creased his face and crinkled his eyes so that all sign of sadness was gone. His hair, smooth and brown was cut fairly short but the style suited him, emphasising the strength of his jaw. He looked dependable and for a moment Tara had to fight hard to overcome the temptation to tell him the truth about Paul. She would feel so much safer if there was someone else who knew the dangers that threatened Paul; if someone else, preferably someone like Steven, was on hand should Simon Hamilton turn up on his release. She realised now the temptation to which Mrs Ward had succumbed when she had poured out the whole tale to Tara, but remembering her promise to keep the confidence Tara now said nothing more on the subject, and was relieved when the conversation turned to other things.

'What about that drink?' suggested Steven.

'I'm afraid there's no licence here,' said Tara 'and I can't leave the house with Paul asleep upstairs.'

'No, of course not,' agreed Steven. 'But I've a bottle of scotch upstairs in my room. Shall I bring it down?'

Tara grinned, feeling conspiratorial and nodded. Steven went upstairs and returned a moment later with the bottle, and it was only a matter of moments before they were settled comfortably in the two kitchen arm-chairs, each nursing a large scotch on the rocks, and chatting easily like old friends. Tara, eager to keep the subject away from Paul's family, asked Steven about himself, his holiday, and they were soon on to the subject of boats which appeared to be his overriding passion.

'There's one coming in here in a few days time,' he said, 'I'm not quite sure when she's due, but I'm hoping to get a look at her. She's supposed to be coming up for sale and I want to give her the once over before anyone knows I'm interested in buying.'

At last Tara yawned and said, 'I'm sorry I shall have to go up to bed. It's an early start again in the morning and I mustn't oversleep. Thanks for the drink.'

'Pleasure,' smiled Steven. 'I think I'll take a walk, stretch my legs before I go to bed. I'll see you in the morning.'

Tara gave him a guest's front door key and they parted in the hall and having checked the ground floor doors and windows Tara stumbled upstairs, suddenly aware of her exhaustion. She was soon undressed and comfortably in her bed, and it was not until she was about to switch off her light, that she remembered her promise to Paul. She paused with her hand on the switch. Must she really get up again and go and sleep in his grandmother's room? She was sorely tempted to remain where she was, but recalling the child's trembling lip she swung her legs out of bed and reached for her dressing gown. She would feel dreadful if Paul awoke and she were not there as she had promised. Quietly she opened her bedroom door. The dimmed lights burned on the landing as always and she crept up the next flight of stairs to Mrs Ward's room. Without putting the light on she slipped between the sheets and snuggled down again. She left the door ajar so that Paul could call if he needed her and hoping he would not, she plunged into the depths of sleep.

4

Quite what woke her sometime later, Tara did not know, nor how long she was in the limbo of half-sleep before she was aware she was truly awake and not dreaming, but sounds gradually penetrated her consciousness and she realised she was not alone in the room. She sat up, rubbing her eyes.

'Paul! Is that you?'

The room was in complete darkness and she realised the door was now shut. Footsteps crossed quickly to the window. As Tara fumbled for the unfamiliar bedside light, she heard the rasp of the curtains thrown back and saw the shape of a man, silhouetted for a moment against the window.

Tara cried out and grabbing again for the bedside lamp only succeeded in knocking it on to the floor. She struggled out of bed to the door and switched on the main light, one glance showed the sash window thrown open and the man gone. Paul! He must have been after Paul, and come into the wrong room. Tara flung open the door and dived across the landing into Paul's room, switching on his light as she did so. Woken by the sudden brightness, Paul sat up in bed, rubbing his eyes, confused.

'Paul, are you all right?' Tara spoke a little shakily; but Paul appeared not to notice and answered in surprise, 'Tara. I'm okay. Why?'

Hastily Tara regained her control. 'Sorry if I woke you, Paul. I thought I heard you call out. I must have been dreaming.'

Determined not to cause the boy any further alarm she settled him down again and tucked him in.

'Go back to sleep, Paul. I'll see you in the morning. Don't worry, I'm next door as I promised.'

But Tara did not go back to bed in Mrs Ward's room. First she peered out of the bedroom window, to discover how the man escaped. That was easy to see, there was a little wrought iron balcony outside both her and Paul's windows and between them was a white-painted drainpipe. Below, the garden was in darkness, but once safely down, the intruder could slip out of the door in the grey stone wall and be clear away in no time. The man must have come up that drainpipe and mistaken which window was Paul's. The intruder must have been Paul's father. He had discovered where the boy was and come to get him. Panic flooded through Tara as she realised how easily the man had gained access to Old Court.

'I must tell the police,' she muttered out loud, and sliding the window closed she pushed the catch across so that there was no chance of anyone entering Old Court that way again; then creeping across the landing she stole downstairs to the telephone. All was silent in the guest house. Tara glanced at her watch. Two o'clock. Should she phone now, even though there was no chance of catching the man, and so disturb the entire place, and worry the guests into the bargain, or should she wait until morning?

She stood poised on the first floor landing, wondering whether to go on down or return to bed, when on sudden impulse she turned aside and knocked on Steven Harris's door. There was no reply and Tara tapped again more loudly. This time he called her to come in and as she opened the door he switched on his bedside lamp.

'Tara!' he said, rubbing the sleep from his eyes. 'What on earth's the matter? You look as white as a sheet.'

'Steven, I'm sorry to wake you, only . . .' she paused as she felt tears prick her eyes.

'Tara, whatever is wrong? You're shivering. Here, put this round you.' Steven had got out of bed and scooping up the eiderdown he had earlier discarded on to the floor, he wrapped it round her and pushed her gently to sit on the bed.

Tara, grateful for the warmth of the eiderdown, and a little unnerved by the gentleness in Steven's voice tried again.

'I'm sorry to disturb you, Steven, only we've had an intruder and I don't know what to do.'

'Call the police,' replied Steven, promptly.

'I know I should,' said Tara, 'but he's gone now and it'll disturb everyone in the house.'

'Even so, they ought to be informed as soon as possible, they might pick him up round the town.'

'I suppose so,' sighed Tara.

'Tell me what happened,' suggested Steven, seeing that she was not quite convinced.

So Tara told him, though she still did not mention Paul's father.

'What do you think he was after?' asked Steven, puzzled by her edited version of the story.

'Me,' said a little voice and they both

swung round to find the pyjama-ed figure of Paul standing in the doorway.

'It was my father, after me, wasn't it, Tara?' His lip trembled and he burst into tears.

Tara struggled free of the eiderdown and gathered him into her arms. The child clung to her sobbing and Steven stared at the two of them quite uncomprehending.

'It's all right, Paul,' Tara soothed. 'It's all right. We don't know that it was your father, it could well have been an ordinary burglar who saw an open window and shinned up the drainpipe to take a chance.'

'You don't know,' cried the child. 'Gran said he'd gone away, but Uncle Andrew said he might come.'

'Uncle Andrew has a great deal to answer for,' snapped Tara furious at this unknown uncle who had so frightened the boy.

'Would somebody please explain what is going on?' demanded Steven, staring down at Tara with the boy still clasped in her arms.

The time for pretence was over, Steven should now be told of the danger to Paul and Tara found it a great relief to tell him. He listened in silence and when she had finished he turned to Paul and said, 'Well, old son, there's nothing more for you to worry about. We shan't let anyone carry you off or harm you in any way, shall we, Tara? I doubt, actually, if you've much to fear from your father. It sounds to me as if your Gran has let her fears get out of hand, but don't worry. Tara and I will be here until Gran gets back to look after you again.' He picked the boy up in his arms and said, 'Now, back to bed with you. We're both here. It won't look nearly so bad in the morning. Say night night to Tara, and up we'll go.'

Tara was still sitting on the end of Steven's bed when he came down again. She had wrapped the eiderdown round her again and sat wondering what to do next. The relief at not having to shoulder the burden of fear alone far outweighed the sneaking guilt she felt at having broken Mrs Ward's confidence and told Steven everything; but although he had promised Paul that he and Tara would look after him until Mrs Ward came home, she knew he would not stay that long. Once the boat he was waiting for arrived, he would be off on business of his own. Still, in the meantime she was glad the truth was out.

Steven returned to find her sitting where he had left her. 'I don't know if he'll sleep again for a bit, but he's tucked up in bed, and I've checked that his window's latched.'

'Thank you, Steven.' Weariness overcame Tara and she longed for her own bed. 'What about the police?'

Steven considered for a moment. 'Well,' he said, 'there probably isn't much point in calling them now. It's a good half hour since you woke up. Nothing was taken, was it?'

'I don't know. I've no idea what Mrs Ward has in her room.'

'I think you'd better ring them to be on the safe side.' He looked at her, her eyes enormous in her pale face and said, 'You phone them and I'll make a cup of tea to warm you up, unless you'd rather have something stronger.'

'No, tea, please,' said Tara. Unwrapping the eiderdown she realised for the first time that she was dressed only in her pale green nightdress, which left little to the imagination. She blushed and as casually as she could, said, 'I'll just get my dressing gown and slippers.'

Steven grinned. 'Pity,' he said, 'but you're probably right, we don't want you down with pneumonia.'

They sat in the kitchen drinking their tea waiting for the police to arrive.

'What should I say about Paul's father?' Tara asked Steven.

'That depends on how much credence you give to the idea that it was him.'

'I don't know. I can't really believe he'd go to those lengths, whatever Mrs Ward said and Paul believes. We've no evidence, and yet I must admit it was my first thought when I realised someone had broken in.'

'How would he have got Paul out? He could hardly shin down a drainpipe with him on his back?'

'I suppose he might have risked carrying him out through the house.'

'He might. Would you?'

Tara smiled and Steven whose question had been intended to provoke that smile was pleased.

'No. Certainly not against Paul's will.'

'He could have drugged him, I suppose?' hazarded Steven with a gleam in his eyes.

Tara laughed this time. 'Perhaps I won't mention Paul's father just yet. It does seem ludicrous when considered rationally.'

'Don't get me wrong,' said Steven earnestly, 'I'm not underestimating your fears, or Paul's, or Mrs Ward's for that matter, but I do tend to think they are probably unfounded. Let's think again. When you woke up, what was the man doing?'

'Doing? I don't know, it was dark.'

'Well, where was he in the room?'

'By the cupboard. There's a big dormer cupboard built in under the roof. He had a torch.'

'Was the door open, the cupboard door I mean, when you finally got the light on?'

'Yes, I think it was ajar.'

'And when you woke up and heard something did you see the torch immediately?'

Tara thought for a moment and then said, 'No, not at once.'

'So he could have been in the cupboard.'

'I suppose so.'

'I doubt if he thought Paul was in a cupboard.'

Tara laughed. 'You're right. I hadn't given any thought to what he was actually doing, I just jumped to what seemed to be the obvious conclusion.'

'Easily done,' agreed Steven.

The door bell rang, the police had arrived.

It was daylight by the time Tara was finally able to creep back into bed. The police listened to her factual account of the night's events and then inspected the window and drainpipe, peered into the dormer cupboard, it's door still ajar, looked at the courtyard and garden door and agreed that the questioning of the guests who were undisturbed could wait until morning. She locked the front door behind them and followed Steven upstairs. He was waiting on the landing and as she reached him he took her hand and said, 'Anyone ever tell you how gorgeous you look in a nightie?'

'Steven!' expostulated Tara, laughing.

'Goodnight, Tara.' He released her hand and turned into his room, leaving Tara to climb the stairs to Mrs Ward's room once more, exhausted but strangely light-hearted after such an ominously eventful evening.

The police returned in the morning

and discreetly made their enquiries among the guests. Only three had had late keys and even these were all sound asleep before Tara discovered the intruder. The guests' bedrooms were all on the first floor and none had heard anything of the evening's events.

'Sound sleepers, your customers,' remarked the constable as he snapped his note book closed.

Tara shrugged. 'Must be the air or something.'

'Well, we'll let you know if we get anywhere,' went on the policeman. 'Nothing in the courtyard, but that's not surprising. Garden gate was open.'

'I'm afraid it often is,' said Tara. 'It's constantly used by the guests and ourselves as a short cut to the beach.'

The constable nodded. 'Well, as I said, we'll be in touch if we get a line on him, and if you find anything missing or remember anything else, perhaps you'll let us know.'

It was on the tip of Tara's tongue to tell him about Paul's father then, she even raised her hand as she moved to call him back, but thinking she was waving to him the young constable lifted his hand in reply and climbing into his panda car, drove away. The call died on her lips and Tara turned back into Old Court to get on with the morning's chores.

The next few days passed in a sort of dream. Each day immediately after breakfast, Tara rang the hospital, but there was no change in Mrs Ward's condition. She went to visit her on two occasions, leaving Paul with Steven, but on neither was she allowed to do more than peep round the door at the unmoving figure in the bed.

A great deal of hard work was needed to keep Old Court running efficiently, but Tara, no longer bound by Mrs Ward's rather rigid routine, found several ways of, as Steven put it, increasing productivity. Often it was with his help and this meant the afternoons were free to take Paul out, and relax for a few hours. On the day after the night visitor, Steven had joined an expedition they had made to a miniature zoo and pets' corner and the outing was such a success that from then on he was included in all their plans, and the expeditions became the high-spot of everyone's day.

'What about this boat?' Tara asked him one day. 'Aren't you supposed to be seeing that, rather than jaunting round the countryside with us?'

They were sitting in a cottage tea garden having just demolished an enormous pile of scones topped with raspberry jam and cream and relaxing over a second pot of tea while Paul explored the village green across the road.

'I'm waiting for a phone call,' replied Steven idly stirring more sugar into his tea. 'My friend'll call when they get here.' He changed the subject. 'When you've finished tonight can I take you out to dinner?'

Tara's heart leapt. She would enjoy spending time with Steven without Paul as a perpetual chaperone. Several times she had had an irrational desire to touch Steven, to take his hand, trace the line of his smile with her finger or smooth the hair from his forehead, but he had made no move towards her since the night of the intruder and she had come to the decision that although each was completely at ease in the company of the other, and a friendship had developed, the physical attraction she felt for Steven was not returned. However, now he had actually suggested they go out alone she felt hope stirring, but equally she knew she could not accept, because, as always, of Paul.

'Oh, Steven, I'd love to, but I can't leave Paul.'

'Supposing I get a babysitter?'

'But he won't know her.'

'He probably won't even see her. He'll be asleep before she comes.'

'Suppose he wakes,' objected Tara.

'He won't. He hasn't woken for three or four nights now, has he? If I run him off his feet on the beach before supper he'll crash the moment he gets into bed.'

Tara was still dubious.

'Where will you get a sitter from? We don't know anyone.'

'I'll get one,' said Steven firmly. 'Now, will you come? Please?' His eyes held hers for a moment.

'All right,' agreed Tara, 'if you can get a reliable sitter. Not a schoolgirl of fifteen mind, a proper responsible person.'

'You're on. Now, let's start the wearing out process.' Steven got to his feet. 'Paul! Do you want to play some football?'

'Steve's fun, isn't he, Tara?' said Paul, as she saw him into bed several hours later. 'We played lots of football and he made me a long jump pit on the beach. Tomorrow he says we can go and look at the boats. He knows how to sail and he says he'll teach me.'

Tara hugged him. 'That's marvellous, but you mustn't mind if you don't manage to fit everything in before he goes home. He's only on holiday, remember.'

And remember it yourself, she admonished her reflection in the glass as she paid extra attention to her make-up. Holiday romance is all he has in mind, and all you should have, too. Enjoy the fun, he's good company and most attractive, but keep a firm hand on the emotions, for they won't come into play.

She stood back from the mirror on the little wardrobe door to admire herself. Her hair hung loose at her shoulders and shone in the lamplight; her simple green dress picked up the colour of her eyes which were already lit with the sparkle of excitement.

'Miss Dereham,' she murmured, 'though you say it yourself, you look stunning.' And laughing at herself, she thought, That's the spirit, laugh, enjoy yourself and keep your feet on the ground, and with this final reminder she looked in on Paul, now fast asleep and went downstairs to greet Mrs Carr, sent by a local agency to baby-sit.

'She was perfect,' Tara told Steven as

they walked into town. 'Just what I asked for.'

'Oh, I was most specific in my request,' said Steven seriously. 'Someone fat and fifty, I told them, with grey hair and a motherly bosom!'

'Exact in every respect' cried Tara.

'Oh, and I also said someone who didn't mind going to bed late,' Steven went on. 'You need a complete change and this evening is going to be it.'

'Come on then,' laughed Tara, still buoyed with confidence by the look of admiration she had caught in Steven's eyes as she came downstairs. 'I bet you fall asleep before I do.'

5

It was a perfect late summer evening, the sky still a clear gold over the sea as the dusk crept through the town and the faintest breeze stirred the leaves on the palm trees in the beach gardens. Steven had not only arranged for the matronly Mrs Carr to come and baby-sit, but had booked a table at Corrado's, an attractive Italian restaurant in one of the twisting side streets so characteristic of the older part of Silverstrand. After an excellent meal complete with wine, soft lights and guitarist they sampled one of Silverstrand's summer night clubs; but the music was strident and the lights garish and they did not stay.

'I must be getting old,' declared Tara as they battled their way out into the cool night air again. 'I used to haunt places like that.'

Steven laughed. 'Definitely incipient old age,' he agreed. 'I shan't admit it, but isn't it nice to be out here!' and laughing together they wandered on to the beach.

A full moon hung low in the sky, a huge yellow disc creeping clear of the horizon, leaving a faint yellow trail across the water. Tara carried her green sandals dangling from her hand as with fingers linked they strolled at the water's edge watching the waves exploding silver on the tide-smoothed sand.

It was inevitable, Tara supposed, that Steven should kiss her, indeed she had been looking forward to that moment, certain it would come; yet when he did gently, lingeringly, she felt, dare she admit it even to herself, disappointed! There was no demanding passion in his lips, just a tenderness, perhaps brought on by the wine and the moonlight or perhaps Steven, too, felt the strange inevitability, or even worse, that he must kiss her because she expected it.

Her mind had been warning her all evening, No emotional involvement. Enjoy kissing him, but don't let your heart join in, but she knew her heart had been ready to ignore that admonition.

'I've wanted to do that from the moment I saw you coming downstairs all flustered that first morning,' said Steven softly when he raised his head at last.

'You should have done it sooner,' teased Tara.

'Shameless hussy,' he grinned and kissed her again.

Tara returned his kisses as before, but somehow there was something indefinable missing and she felt cheated. She wondered if Steven did, too, but he gave no sign. A wind sprang up with the turn of the tide and Tara shivered.

'Let's go for a final coffee before we go home.'

'Isn't everywhere shut now?' asked Tara, surprised. 'It's awfully late.'

'I know a place that isn't,' said

Steven. 'Come on, I'll show you.' He took her to a late night coffee stall outside the pier and bought them each coffee served in thick white china mugs. Sitting on the sea wall with their feet dangling they nursed their coffees in harmonious silence and when they had finished, walked back to Old Court in complete accord.

'Had a good evening?' enquired Mrs Carr as she shrugged her shapeless coat over her motherly bosom.

'Lovely, thank you,' answered Tara, trying not to catch Steven's eye as she watched Mrs Carr's manoeuvres.

'The little boy didn't wake,' went on Mrs Car. 'Haven't heard a sound all evening,' and when Steven had paid her she disappeared into the night. Tara closed the door behind her and made her usual round of doors and windows before going up to bed. Steven waited for her in the hall and it crossed Tara's mind that he might be hoping to spend the night with her. Earlier, as she had been getting ready to go out it had seemed a distinct possibility and one she had prepared herself to accept, but now she was almost certain she would sleep alone. On the landing Steven took her in his arms once more and kissed her as he had before, but when she thanked him for a lovely evening and said goodnight he made no move to follow her into her room.

Tara flopped on her bed and gazing up at the ceiling considered the evening. Where had it changed? She had been so happy when he had suggested they went out, so aware of him beside her as they sat at dinner and walked on the beach. His smile captivated her, his laugh was infectious, his physical presence made her tingle, but then when he kissed her there was obviously nothing more than a gentle pleasure on either side. Tara smiled ruefully to herself and forced herself to make the effort to undress and crawl into bed.

The jangle of the alarm dragged her back to consciousness next morning, but it was several minutes before she could bring herself to leave the snug warmth of her bed to face another day of breakfasts, lunches and suppers. Since Steven had proved so ready to help Tara had made no effort to find an assistant; but today she really must, she decided, for Steven would not be there for ever, and nor, come to think of it would she; the agency was far too expensive to use as more than a stop gap, and Mrs Ward would need somebody permanent if and when she came out of hospital.

The serving of breakfast which always kept Tara on her toes was made even more chaotic that morning by the hospital telephoning in the middle of it to say that Mrs Ward had regained consciousness and wanted to see her. On hearing of the call Steven offered to take Paul out for the day to allow Tara to sort out the guest house. It was Saturday which meant there were no lunches that day as it was changeover day. Almost all the guests were leaving and would be gone by eleven and a new lot would be arriving from three o'clock onwards. If she kept going at top speed, Tara reckoned she would be able to visit the hospital before the next people arrived.

She arrived there soon after one and was allowed in to see Mrs Ward immediately.

'She's still very ill,' the nurse warned Tara. 'She's virtually paralysed down her right side and though she can talk quite well she doesn't always maintain a train of thought through to the end.'

Tara nodded and crept into the side cubicle where Mrs Ward lay. Paul's card was displayed on the locker and the bunch of flowers she had brought herself last time was in a vase beside it. Today she had brought nothing with her except the mail which had accumulated since Mrs Ward had been taken ill, and when she saw how pale and small the old lady looked lying alseep in the big hospital bed she regretted that she had even brought that.

Quietly she crossed to the bedside and sat in the chair set there. After a moment or two Mrs Ward opened her eyes. She gazed up at the ceiling without registering the fact that she had a visitor.

'Mrs Ward,' Tara whispered, bending towards the bed, and speaking softly so as not to alarm her. Mrs Ward tried to move her head, her eyes straining to see who was sitting beside her.

'Don't try to move, Mrs Ward. It's me, Tara Dereham.'

There was no comprehension in the old lady's face.

'Tara Dereham?' she repeated.

'Remember, I came to help you run the guest house, to help with Old Court? Paul sends his love.'

That did penetrate her brain and she said, 'Paul. Is Paul all right? Paul. My little Paul.' She reached out agitatedly with her left hand as if searching for him.

Alarmed Tara took her hand and said, 'Paul's fine, just fine. He sends his love. Don't get upset, Mrs Ward, there's nothing for you to worry about. I'm looking after him.'

'Must look after Paul.'

'I am; I promise.'

'The hotel? What about the hotel?'

'That's fine, too,' said Tara reassuringly. 'It's changeover day today. They all said what a lovely holiday they'd had and they're going to come back next year.' Tara neglected to mention the intruder and the police questioning of the guests the next morning. No progress had been made in finding the man and there seemed little chance he would ever be found. There was no point in agitating Mrs Ward with it until she was well on the mend.

'I've brought your letters, Mrs Ward. Shall I leave them on your locker?'

'Open, please.'

'Shall I read them to you?'

'You answer. May be bookings.'

'Well, if I open them now and just scan through, if there's anything I can't cope with you can tell me what to do.'

She flipped through the pile of envelopes, setting aside obvious bills and then began to open those she had left. Two were enquiries about Old Court's terms, one was a circular, one was confirming a booking and the last was from a London solicitor. It was typewritten and Tara did not immediately look at the signature, but when she grasped the import of the contents of the letter her eyes flicked to the bottom of the page and saw the name scrawled there. '*Andrew.*' In the list of partners on the notepaper heading was one '*Andrew V. Harper.*'

'This one's from Andrew' she began carefully. 'He's a little worried . . . '

'Read it, please.'

Tara wondered whether to paraphrase what Andrew had written as it was sure to worry Mrs Ward, yet she felt that knowing too little might make her worry more than knowing it all.

'All right,' she agreed at last, 'but you mustn't let it upset you, because there's no need. He says,' Tara consulted the letter again, and then read it out loud.

'Dear Mrs W.,

'Just a line to warn you that Simon Hamilton was released ten days ago. I would have written before but only found the notification here on my return from holiday. He does not know where you and Paul are living but he may find a way to trace you and if he does I'm sure you can expect a visit from him. Give me a call as soon as you get this letter if you are worried at all. I'll try to get down to see you and we can plan our campaign. As we have said before there is the possibility of his trying to kidnap Paul, so if he does show his face don't leave him alone with the boy.

'My best to you and Paul.
'Andrew.'

There was a moan from the bed and Mrs Ward closed her eyes. Tara took one look at her chalky face and rang the bedside bell.

When the nurse came in and saw the letters opened on the bed she turned to Tara angrily.

'What have you been bothering the poor dear with? She's too ill to deal with letters.'

Tara did not bother to explain it all, but murmured, 'I'm sorry,' and drew away from the bed to allow the nurse closer to take Mrs Ward's pulse. The old lady opened her eyes again and straining to see Tara, asked for her loudly and petulantly.

'Tara. I want Tara.'

Tara went back to the bedside.

'I'm here, don't worry.'

'Ring Andrew. Must come. Andrew must come.'

'I will. I'll phone as soon as I get back to Old Court. Don't worry, he'll come.'

The nurse motioned Tara away from the bed again and Mrs Ward closed her eyes, still muttering, 'Must ring Andrew. Must come Andrew.' then suddenly there was silence.

'She's asleep now,' said the nurse, smoothing the covers over the old lady and tucking her arm in comfortably beneath them.

'Do you know what she wants you to do?'

'Yes, I'm to phone her solicitor.'

'Oh, I see,' said the nurse. 'Probably wants to change her will. Often do that at the last minute.'

'Is it the last minute?' asked Tara seriously.

The nurse smiled reassuringly. 'She may well make a good recovery,' she said. 'We must hope so, but it'll be a long haul back. Get the solicitor here, it'll no doubt be a worry off her mind.'

Tara was not so sure of that, but still clutching all the letters she had brought with her, she went slowly out to the car park considering what to do next. Perhaps the best thing to do was to phone this Andrew, though what little she had heard of him from Paul did nothing to endear him to her. But, at least he could advise her as to what to do if Paul's father did succeed in tracing him; how she could protect the child and what legal right she had, if any, to stop Simon Hamilton removing Paul there and then.

6

Old Court was quiet and still when Tara let herself in. A quick glance at the clock told her she had a little over half an hour before the next lot of guests might start arriving. Telephoning Andrew Harper, she decided must be the first job, and she took out his letter to discover his telephone number. She re-read the letter and then with a slight feeling of apprehension dialled the number printed on the top. There was no reply. Tara let the number ring for several minutes before finally replacing the receiver.

'Of course,' she cried in frustration, 'it's Saturday afternoon. There won't be anyone in a solicitor's office on a Saturday afternoon.'

She sunk down on to a chair and pondered what to do. Should she wait until Monday morning and phone

Andrew at his office again, or should she go back to the hospital in the hope Mrs Ward could give her his home number? There was no private phone book beside the telephone, there were the post office local directories, though none of course for the London area, where Andrew Harper lived. Then Tara remembered the handbag, Mrs Ward's capacious black handbag. She had noticed it under the table by the bed in the old lady's bedroom. Perhaps she kept friends' phone numbers in her diary. It was worth a look, particularly as Tara did not relish either of the other possibilities.

Running quickly up to Mrs Ward's bedroom she found the bag and sitting down on the bed she rummaged through it in search of a diary. The bag was crammed with bits and pieces and in the end Tara found it easier to tip everything out on to the bed. In among the letters, handkerchiefs, cheque book, bank book, keys and various other necessities she unearthed the diary and flicking through it found at the end a list of telephone numbers, and amongst them were two marked 'Andrew (home)' and 'Andrew (office)'. Hurriedly Tara stuffed everything back into the handbag, dropping the bunch of keys in her haste. As she retrieved them from the floor she noticed a red plastic label, which obviously belonged to one of the keys, had snapped off and was loose. Picking it up Tara read the words 'JANE'S BOX' neatly printed on it. She looked at the bunch of keys in her hand. She had no idea to which key the label belonged, and having no time to work it out, she simply slipped the keys and the separate label into the bag and pushed the bag back under the table where she had found it. She glanced at the telephone extension by the bed but decided to make the call from the kitchen in case it took a while and the new guests began arriving.

Tara took the diary downstairs with her and returning to the kitchen dialled the number listed as 'Andrew (home)'.

Again there was no reply, and again Tara let it ring for several minutes before accepting the fact that Andrew was not going to answer.

'Damn, damn. Everything seems to be conspiring against me today.'

The doorbell jangled and Tara, seeing it was almost three o'clock, got wearily to her feet to welcome the next wave of Mrs Ward's guests; but by the time she reached the front door it had already swung open to admit the visitor. She had left the door on the latch as it always was during the daytime for the convenience of the guests. The newcomer was very tall, lean and strong, and silhouetted against the afternoon sun, he was dark, his face without features, in shadow. He paused on the threshold and looked her up and down before he spoke.

'Can I help you?' faltered Tara, a little overcome by his silent appraisal. She was about to ask if he had a booking when he said, 'Where's Mrs Ward?'

'I'm afraid Mrs Ward's in hospital.

My name's Tara Dereham. I'm looking after Old Court for her just now. Can I help you?'

'Where's the boy?' snapped the man ignoring her question. 'Where's Paul?'

Tara stared at him and a terrible realisation came over her. The worst had happened, Simon Hamilton had found them and had come to take Paul.

Play it cool; feign ignorance of the situation; bluff it out. That's what she must do, but it was easier thought than done. However, determined not to be overawed by Paul's father, Tara braced herself mentally and said politely — 'Paul? I'm afraid he's out for the day with a friend. He'll be back later. Have you a booking or were you just looking in to visit Mrs Ward?'

The man came right into the hall and closed the front door behind him.

'What's the matter with her?' he asked brusquely.

'You said she's in hospital.'

'I'm afraid she's had a stroke. It's left

her paralysed down the right hand side of her body.'

'Who's looking after the boy?' demanded the man.

'I am,' replied Tara crisply. 'I am well aware of the situation and I shall keep Paul safely here unless or until his grandmother tells me different.'

'If you know 'the situation' as you put it, why the hell didn't you contact me the moment Mrs Ward was taken ill?'

'Contact you?' Tara was incredulous.

'Of course, it would seem to be the obvious thing to have done. I'm a family friend as well as being her solicitor.'

Tara stared at him and as her brain registered what he had just said she felt weak-kneed with relief. She dropped on to the hall chair and said weakly, 'You're Andrew Harper.'

'Of course. Who did you think I was?'

'I thought,' said Tara colouring a little at the admission, 'I thought you were Simon Hamilton.'

Andrew Harper gave a shout of laughter.

'Me? Simon Hamilton?'

'I thought you'd come to try and take Paul away.'

He laughed again and Tara said, angrily defensive, 'It's not so funny; it certainly wouldn't have been if you had been Paul's father. You march in here demanding to see Mrs Ward and Paul, without any introduction or even giving your name. How on earth am I expected to know who you are?' She leapt to her feet as she spoke and Andrew Harper held out his hands as if to fend her off.

'Sorry, sorry,' he cried. 'I wasn't thinking, I'm so used to walking in here unannounced. Now, suppose we start again over a cup of coffee and you can tell me all about it?'

Somewhat mollified Tara led him through into the kitchen and made some coffee; and as they drank it together at the table Tara told him the whole story.

'I suggested Mrs Ward applied to an agency for help,' said Andrew. 'She rang me in a bit of a panic before I went on holiday. That was three weeks ago.'

'Well, I've been here just over two weeks,' said Tara, 'and it's all been fairly hectic. The intruder was the last straw. I haven't told Mrs Ward about him yet; she's got enough on her mind, particularly since she had your letter this morning. I've been trying to get hold of you ever since; to ask you to come down and see her.'

'Well, it's lucky I came. I'll go and see her later on. Tell me more about your midnight visitor. Have the police come up with anything?'

Tara sighed. 'Not yet; they say it happens all the time during the season; sneak thieves in and out for some quick pickings. It did cross my mind it was Paul's father, but, well, it's a bit unlikely really. I mean, he'd try the direct approach first, wouldn't you think?'

'Did you tell the police?'

'That it might be Simon Hamilton?

No, I didn't. There was no evidence. After all the man seemed to be looking in the cupboard. I thought it would just complicate matters.'

'Hmm!'

Tara could see Andrew Harper thought that she should have at least voiced her suspicions and left it to the police to sort out; but before either of them could say more the door bell jangled again announcing the arrival of a family to begin its stay at Old Court Guest House and Tara had to hurry out to welcome them.

For the rest of the afternoon she had little time to give to Andrew Harper. She was expecting a full house for dinner, according to Mrs Ward's book-ings diary, and she had to keep leaving her preparations to greet new arrivals and show them to their rooms. Andrew had decided that he would stay for a few days to help out and try to engage some permanent help. He installed himself in Mrs Ward's room; the only one that was free.

'You wouldn't consider staying on through the winter, would you?' he asked Tara hopefully.

'I doubt if Mrs Ward could afford the agency fees,' she replied, peeling potatoes to go with the evening's pork chops.

'I didn't mean as an agency employee, but as a permanent job — a sort of nanny-housekeeper. Both Paul and his grandmother are going to need looking after. We'd find someone else to help out, of course, but you could take charge.'

Tara shook her head. 'I like doing my agency work,' she said, 'it's always so varied. This is fine for a few weeks, but I shouldn't want to do it for more than that.'

Andrew sighed. 'Pity,' he said, 'you'd have been perfect. Still, let me know if you change your mind.'

But as Tara set the tables in the dining room, showed the guests to their rooms and bundled up towels and sheets for the laundry man to collect on Monday, she was determined to leave it all behind as soon as Andrew Harper could find a suitable replacement. She felt a twinge at the prospect of saying goodbye to Paul. In the time she had been there she had become very fond of him and worried for him because of the bitterness in his life and the fears with which he had to contend. Still, now Andrew Harper had turned up to take charge, she could leave the worrying and the precautions to him. In a way it would be a relief if Paul's father did appear, at least they would know where they stood.

Tara thought he probably would come one day; she knew if it were she who had lost her child as he had, she would make every effort to find him; unless of course Mrs Ward was right and he really did not care. But if that were so why was the old lady so afraid he would come? If he really did not care he would be glad to be free of the responsibility.

'Not my problem, thank goodness,' Tara remarked to the air.

'What isn't?' Andrew Harper had

appeared at the kitchen door.

Tara blushed at being caught talking to herself and said, 'I was thinking about Paul and his father.'

'Oh, I see. Well I'm off to the hospital now to see if I can see Mrs Ward. Can you keep me some dinner if I get held up?'

'Yes, of course. You'll find Mrs Ward ... ' began Tara, but was interrupted by Paul bursting into the room, shrieking with excitement.

'Tara, Tara! Steven took me sailing. We hired a boat and I wore a life-jacket and we went sailing.' Then he saw Andrew and went on, 'Uncle Andrew, I've been sailing, on the sea. Steven took me. He's a good sailor, he's going to teach me, he says ... ' the child's voice tailed off to silence as he caught sight of Andrew Harper's face. Steven was framed in the kitchen doorway and for a long minute the two men stared at each other, Steven's face strangely expressionless while Andrew's emotions chased across his brow, unchecked fury, fear, contempt and fury again before he schooled his features to disdain. Tara watched them both in stunned silence, completely apart, apparently completely forgotten.

'I wondered how long it would be before you turned up,' said Andrew, his voice soft with barely suppressed rage.

'But you knew I would, Harper. You knew I'd catch up with you in the end.' Steven sounded calm but there was an edge to his voice liked honed steel.

Paul stared at them both frightened by the naked hostility.

'Uncle Andrew, Steven, I don't understand.'

Andrew turned to him and said, 'No, of course you don't, my boy; let me introduce you. That man is your father, Paul. That man is Simon Hamilton.'

Paul turned deathly pale, his little body rigid as he gripped the table.

'I don't believe you!' he shouted, 'I don't believe you. That's Steven. He's my friend. He's going to teach me to sail.'

His voice faded to uncertainty as

Steven crossed the room to him and dropping down beside him placed his hands on the boy's shoulders.

'It's true, Paul,' he began gently, 'I am your father. I wanted — '

Paul broke away violently from his clasp and turning on them screamed at them, tears streaming down his face. 'I hate you! I hate you all!' and rushing from the kitchen he flung himself upstairs to the safe familiarity of his own bedroom.

Tara was scarcely less thunderstruck than Paul. She stared at the two men glowering at each other and the anger boiled inside her. Duped by Steven, despised by Andrew she turned on them both.

'You bastards!' Her voice was low and her words distinctly spoken. 'You bastards. Neither of you gives a damn about that child. You just play off your petty jealousies with him as the ball, to be hit in any direction so you can score off each other.' Then without looking further at either of them she followed Paul.

7

Paul's door was locked when she reached his room, but through its thickness Tara could hear the little boy sobbing, dry, heaving sobs, far beyond the relief of tears. Gently she rapped on the door and called to him.

'Paul! Paul! It's me, Tara. Let me in.'

'No! Go away!' His voice was fierce and angry.

'Paul, I only want to talk to you. Just for a minute. Will you let me in, please?'

'Go away. I don't want anyone.'

'Paul!' Tara called persuasively. 'I need your help, Paul. Can't I come in?'

'No, no, no,' shrieked the little boy. 'Go away. Go away!'

There was nothing Tara could do to force Paul to open the door and so she decided the best thing was to leave him for a little while; give him time to calm down before she approached him again.

In the meantime she needed a chance to calm down herself before she had to appear smiling to the new guests and serve supper. She went to her own room and following Paul's example, locked her door. Flinging herself on her bed she lay on her back and gazed up at the ceiling reconstructing in her mind the events of the last half hour.

Steven Harris was really Simon Hamilton. That was the first thing to be assimilated; worse still that made him a killer, Jane Hamilton's killer. He was Paul's father and had come there specifically to find his son; no wonder he had been so ready to join them on their afternoon expeditions. Tara gave a bitter laugh.

And I thought he wanted to be with me! That's one in the eye for my ego! This led her on to a yet more unpleasant thought. He had been using her, just so he could win Paul's confidence. He needed her friendship to allow him near his son. But what about the previous evening? Was that all part of the plan to keep her sweet until he could whisk Paul away? No wonder his kisses had lacked something, no wonder! Oh, he had made all the right noises, spinning her along on the tide of her own conceit, but he had obviously been working to one end and one end only, and that was to reach Paul.

Anger and bitterness fought inside her and Tara felt degraded and humiliated. Her thoughts turned to Andrew Harper. She could just imagine what his reaction would be next time he spoke to her; but how on earth could she have known Steven Harris was really Simon Hamilton? No one had ever described him to her, there were certainly no photographs of him about the place, no happy family snaps in this unhappy family. Paul was too young to recognise him and though he had used a name with the same initials as his real name, millions of people had those initials. Well, Andrew damned Harper could do his own dirty work now. If it was not for the thought of Paul's distress as his world crumbled round him she would walk out this evening; that and Mrs Ward lying helpless in hospital. She knew it was not in her to leave either of them, but, she determined, she would give it to Andrew Harper straight, she needed extra help immediately and if he did not provide it she would get it from her own agency and blow the expense. He could jolly well pick up the tab or find someone else completely.

Her angry train of thought was interrupted by a quiet tap on her door. Thinking it might be Paul she called out, 'Who is it?'

'It's me, Steven.'

Taking a leaf from Paul's book Tara shouted, 'Go away.'

'I'm leaving.'

'Good!' answered Tara viciously.

'I'll call you later.'

'Don't bother.' She felt better for having been able to give vent to her anger even in so petty a way, and when she had heard him turn from her door and start downstairs she got up from the bed and washed her hands and face, brushed her hair and renewed her make-up, then feeling more in control of herself and outwardly calm she went downstairs to serve dinner.

There was no one in the kitchen and she set about the evening routine in an aura of unreal stillness.

Andrew appeared in the dining room when she rang the gong and sat at a corner table alone. He made no offer of help as she served the meal and then cleared the tables. He had seen Mrs Ward cope in similar circumstances and it did not appear to cross his mind that Tara might be under any strain; but when the other guests had gone out for the evening or retired to the television room Andrew joined her in the kitchen and propped himself against the dresser, lit a cigarette and watched her scour the pots and pans.

'So much for your keeping Paul well clear of his father,' he remarked conversationally. 'You only pushed them into each others arms.'

'How was I supposed to know he was his father? I'm only the hired help, remember? It was only by chance that I knew anything about it at all! And I'll tell you this,' she went on, now launched upon her prepared speech, 'I shan't stay here another day without proper help. If it weren't for Paul and Mrs Ward I'd have gone already, and if you don't find someone immediately I'll go anyway.'

Andrew listened to her tirade drawing on his black cigar, drawing the smoke deep into his lungs and exhaling it in noxious clouds across the kitchen.

'And you'll put yourself into an early grave smoking those revolting things,' Tara concluded, banging the pans on to the draining board. She tossed him a tea towel and said, 'Here, you can dry these saucepans if you're going to stay in here.'

Andrew caught the tea towel and laid it to one side.

'I'm not staying in here. Make what

arrangements you like about extra help, in the short term anyway. I'm going up to see Paul.'

'He's locked himself into his bedroom,' said Tara. 'He doesn't want to see anyone.'

'Oh, he'll probably have calmed down by now,' replied Andrew casually, 'I'll go and see anyway. He'd probably like some supper. You could be finding something for him when you've finished that.' And Andrew Harper sauntered out of the kitchen leaving Tara fuming once again at his arrogance. She crossed the room and slammed the door behind him. She knew it was childish but the violent action relieved her feelings somewhat and released a little of the tension which had been building up inside her.

She did not return to the sink, but dialled the Distress Call Agency in London and quoting Andrew Harper's authorisation asked for help to be sent immediately.

'If Mandy's free perhaps you could

send her,' she suggested. 'We've worked together before and we get on well. This job is getting more complicated every day so I need someone I know I can work with.'

The Agency agreed, Mandy was free as it happened and provided she was happy about joining Tara she should arrive the next day.

Greatly relieved Tara replaced the receiver and was turning back to the sink when the phone shrilled out beside her. Answering it before it rang a second time Tara said wearily, 'Old Court Guest House. Can I help you?'

'Tara? It's me.'

Recognising Steven's voice Tara was tempted to put down the receiver, but anticipating her action he said quickly, 'Please, don't ring off.' Something in his voice stayed her hand, something in its quietness, its seriousness, and she said brusquely, 'Well?'

Calmly and naturally he asked her to meet him at the end of the garden alley so that they could talk. When Tara hesitated he said softly, 'I'm not going to plead with you, Tara; indeed I'll only ask you once. If you refuse I shan't trouble you again, but before you decide remember you haven't heard my side of the story. The accused is usually allowed to speak in his own defence.

Tara pushed the thought of his being a convicted killer to the edge of her mind; she was still angry about being used in his scheming, but the sudden, irrelevant memory of his smile flashed through her mind and she found herself wanting to give him the chance to explain; after all it would only be fair.

'Will you come?' Steven interrupted her silent consideration.

'Yes; all right,' Tara said quickly. 'When I've finished cleaning up here,' and rang off. She glanced guiltily over her shoulder. No one was there, no one had overheard. The door was still shut and it was possible Andrew had not even heard the phone ring.

She want back to the sink, her mind in a turmoil, amazed at herself for agreeing to meet Steven, and yet even on further reflection unwilling for some reason to change her mind.

Andrew stomped back into the kitchen.

'He doesn't want any supper,' he said abruptly.

'What?' Tara had forgotten all about Paul's supper.

'Paul. He says he doesn't want any supper.'

'Oh, well, I should leave him alone then. I'll have another try later on; but it's no good forcing our selves on the child. He'll probably find things easier to face after a good night's sleep.' She paused a moment and then said, 'Are you going to the hospital to see Mrs Ward?'

Andrew frowned. 'No, not tonight. I'm not leaving this place tonight in case Hamilton comes back. Now he's been rumbled he'll probably try to act quickly. We mustn't let the boy out of our sight.'

'Well, I'll leave all that to you,' said

Tara crisply. 'I'm having nothing more to do with this family and its problems. I'll run the guest house until you can find someone else, but I refuse to become involved in anything more emotional than making beds and planning menus. I've got help coming tomorrow by the way,' and she explained about her conversation with the Distress Call Agency. As she mentioned the telephone she waited for Andrew Harper to ask who had just made the incoming call, but apparently he was unaware of it and he did not.

Tara was surprised to discover she had already invented a return call from the Agency to account for that call and wondered why she was prepared to lie to cover her association with Steven. It had crossed her mind that Andrew had not realised that there was anything more than a guest-guest house relationship between Steven and herself and she decided that this was something on which she would not set him right. After all it made no difference to the situation now and there was no need to advertise that she had ever been played for a fool.

'You'll be here if Paul needs you then,' she went on matter-of-factly, 'there's cold meat and cheese in the fridge if he's hungry.'

'Why, where will you be?' asked Andrew, a shade of suspicion colouring his voice.

'Me? I am going out for a breath of fresh air. I've had this place up to here,' she drew a finger expressively across her throat, 'and I'm going out to clear my head and save my sanity.'

She swept past Andrew and went upstairs. At the turn she stopped and glanced down at him standing dark and brooding in the hall and said, 'I'll look in on Paul first, after that he's all yours.'

Paul did not answer her knock on his door and Tara guessed he had fallen into the sleep of exhaustion. She was pleased. Sleep was a great healer of the mind as well as the body and probably things would not look so black to Paul in the morning. There was a line of light under the door, but he had not turned the key and she was still unable to reach him. Softly she called goodnight in case he was still awake and then went down to her own room. She glanced at her reflection in the mirror. She looked like a ghost, her face pale, her skin like paper against the auburn of her hair. She loosened the scarf so that her hair tumbled round her face, shaking her head, enjoying the sensation of freedom it always gave her; then picking up her jacket she set out to meet Steven.

Andrew was still in the hall as Tara came down.

'Paul's asleep I think,' she said. 'I've got a key. You can lock up then you'll know it has all been done properly. Good night.'

Without waiting for Andrew to reply she went out into the courtyard and passed through into the alley beyond. Closing the door in the wall behind her Tara paused to catch her breath and then straightening her shoulders she walked slowly along the narrow pathway between the high walls, wondering how she should behave with Steven, no, not Steven, Simon she must learn to call him now. She reached the end of the alley and emerged on the promenade. The growing dusk was deepened by the coloured lights in the plane trees and the flashing neon signs of the bars and cafes. People still strolled by taking the summer evening air, couples and groups, at peace on a quiet evening. She saw Steven before he saw her and almost turned back, so remote and alone did he seem waiting by the sea wall. Then he caught sight of her and walked across to meet her, greeting her with a faint smile.

'Thank you for coming,' he said. 'Let's find a place where we can talk.'

8

Steven took her arm and led Tara down on to the beach and turning away from the town headed towards the dunes and the river mouth. Tara was alarmed. She had thought they would find a quiet table in a pub or cafe where there were plenty of people close by, not wander off into the loneliness of the dunes. Simon sensed her fear and stopped. He turned her towards him and solemnly said, 'If I promise I won't murder you, will you relax or shall we just walk in opposite directions and call it a day?'

'Don't be silly!' retorted Tara sharply. 'I said I'd come and talk and I will.' Anger at his taunt steadied her nerves and she went on more calmly, 'But you must agree that the circumstances are a little unusual.'

'Agreed,' said Simon promptly and turned once more towards the empty dunes where they would be neither seen or overheard. As they walked, the silence grew like a wall between them. At length Tara stole a glance at his face. It was really no different from yesterday, except that the laughter had gone. The jaw set firm, determined, the eyes deep set, the nose straight; only his mouth no longer curved into a smile and his expression now caught unaware was strained and worried. Tara's thoughts whirled as she found herself intensely conscious of him striding beside her and she withdrew her eyes. She knew she had been on the edge of falling in love with him and now, it was all so different. Or was it? He was the same man. No, he was not, he was not cheerful Steven Harris, as he had led her to believe, but Simon Hamilton, released from a gaol where he'd been imprisoned for killing his wife. Had he used her as Steven Harris to further his cause as Simon Hamilton? Almost certainly yes.

Her thoughts must have registered on

her face as Simon said suddenly 'Penny for them,' and Tara blushed to know he had been looking at her as earlier she had looked at him; and wondered what her expression had revealed.

'Nothing much,' she replied confused, 'just thinking, that's all.'

Tara was relieved that he seemed to accept her reply and said no more. They walked on in silence.

At last they reached the lip of the dunes where they could shelter from the evening breeze and stare out over the eddying waters of the river slipping silently into the sea.

'Right, Steven — Simon,' began Tara using attack as her defence, 'you wanted to explain, explain.'

'Before I say anything else,' said Simon calmly, 'I want you to promise to listen until I've finished. Agreed?'

Tara nodded, and speaking softly Simon began. He told her first of how he had met and married Jane.

'I had just taken over a little bookshop, bought it with a legacy from my uncle. It wasn't a big business, but it paid its way with a little over and I loved it. I started saving to open another, working day and night; I had no time for anything except my books until I met Jane. She really was the most beautiful creature I had ever seen, with long fair hair, fine like spun silk, the sort of hair to turn any man's head; her eyes were dark blue, almost navy and she had a way of gazing at you with an untouched innocence which made you long to look after her, protect her from the world. Her whole body was beautiful, she moved with the grace of a dancer. She was gay and vital. I loved her instantly and distractedly, and danced attendance on her for months. She blew hot and cold; sometimes loving and gentle, other times off-hand, even callous in her attitude to me. But I didn't mind, I adored her, she was everything I'd dreamed of and I could hardly believe it when she finally agreed to marry me. My happiness was complete because I loved her too much and couldn't see what all her beauty concealed so well, what she kept hidden from everyone until it was too late to escape her clutches, that she was evil, vicious, selfish and grasping. And because her evil nature was so cunningly disguised it affected the lives of everyone who knew her.'

Tara exclaimed, 'Oh, but . . . '

Simon said 'No interruptions, remember?'

Tara subsided again and waited for Simon to take up the thread of his story.

'Gradually, after we were married I began to discover she was not the beautiful innocent I had thought; that was a myth I had created for myself. I noticed how barbed some of her witticisms were at the expense of those I thought were her friends. There were unexplained absences, sometimes days at a time and terrified of appearing too possessive and losing her I asked no questions.' He grimaced and went on, 'That was probably my first big mistake, but she could be so sweet and loving, that I dared not ask where she'd been. Then, of course, whispers began coming back to me from friends who 'thought I ought to know' she was having an affair. They didn't have to tell me. I already knew deep inside though I'd ignored the thought. But once everyone knew I had to face the reality.

'At last I confronted her with it and she cried and begged forgiveness and said she'd been very silly; she said it had been a stupid affair, but that it was all over. I believed her and we made it up, lived happily, apparently, for several weeks. Then she announced she was pregnant, and was going to have an abortion. I was horrified and we had a blazing row about it. I said I had some rights as a father and she taunted me and said, possibly, if I was the father, but as far as she knew it could equally well be any one of a dozen men. I was desperate. I knew our marriage, such as it was, was over, but I wanted to salvage something from the wreck; and heaven help me even then I wanted to keep

115

something of her.'

Simon buried his face in his hands for a moment, rubbing his eyes as if to obliterate the memory. Tara reached for his hand and taking it gently between her own said softly, 'Go on.'

Simon drew a deep breath and continued, 'Well, we made a bargain. We would live apart most of the time but I should not divorce her.'

'Why not?' asked Tara.

Simon shrugged. 'It suited her better, for some reason, to be respectably married.'

'I'd have thought she'd have wanted her freedom.'

'So would I, but she didn't. She agreed to have the baby provided I gave her all the money I had saved. She knew I had several thousand saved towards the second shop.'

'Money? For the baby?'

'No, not for Paul. It was to be made over to her for her sole use, the house was transferred to her name and then on top of that I had to keep the three of us on what I was making. So, you see, I bought Paul. If I hadn't he wouldn't exist now. If she hadn't had that money from me Jane would have had an abortion. He's mine, and I intend to have him.'

'But, Simon, what happened to Jane?'

'She went through with the pregnancy, had Paul as arranged and then Mrs Ward came to live with us and looked after him in the day time, though I saw him at weekends and in the evenings of course. Jane convinced her mother that she had a modelling job which was keeping her busy, necessitated having a flat of her own in London, and paid for all the clothes which filled her wardrobes. It was true to a certain extent, she did do some modelling and was popular in several of the glossies, but it certainly wasn't her only source of income. She left Paul entirely to his grandmother. Mrs Ward has always been the mainstay of Paul's life, and I don't want to take him away from her, but neither will I allow her to take him away from me.'

'Didn't she suspect there was something wrong between Jane and you?'

'Not at first; perhaps she chose to ignore the fact, but gradually she had to face the reality that all was not well, and she told me she was going to talk to Jane, to try and persuade her to come home more often and be more of a mother to Paul. I knew Jane had no interest in Paul whatsoever, except in so far as he was a weapon to use against me, but I hadn't realised how she would set about it. When her mother tackled her about being more with Paul, Jane came back to me and demanded the divorce she had refused before.'

'But why?' asked Tara, puzzled. 'Why now and not before?'

'I didn't know; all I did know was that she was going to get her mother to move in with her and demand sole custody of Paul.'

'But she didn't want him!' Tara exploded.

'No, but I did and she knew it. She

did it to hurt me. Jane was like a small boy destroying a fly, very slowly and very deliberately, first the wings, then the legs and at last cut in two. Maximum pain in others brought her maximum pleasure. She loved seeing people squirm.'

There was no bitterness in Simon's voice as he spoke; his voice was flat, without emotion. He had had four years in prison and the hatred he felt once for Jane had long drained away leaving only determination to put all the misery behind him and to start a new life with his son.

'What did you do? What did you say to her?'

Tara found she was feeling the anger missing in Simon and she spoke demandingly.

'Do? I went to see her. In her flat.'

He turned suddenly to Tara showing the first real emotion since he had started to speak.

'I didn't kill her, Tara, not even accidentally, though I came near to it.'

Tara was still holding his hand in hers and she said quietly, 'Tell me what happened.'

Simon sighed. 'I went up to see her and she told me to come in and poured me a drink, all very civilised. Then I told her she could have the divorce, but not Paul. She laughed, and told me to go back to my books. I kept my temper and told her she was no fit mother for my son, she was nothing but a whore. She laughed again and said in that deadly sweet tone of hers, 'But a very high class one, darling. You must admit that. You should meet some of my clients!'. Then she went on, 'It really is most touching to see you so concerned about a snotty kid who probably isn't even your own. I can look it up for you like and tell you who else he might belong to. I keep detailed records you know; so much more fun looking back that way. Dates, performance. Everyone has a record card. Like to see yours? I'll look it up and let you have a list of possible fathers for Paul.'

'It was then that I hit her, full across the face with the flat of my hand. She was so amazed that for a moment she just stared then she launched herself at me, ripping at my face with her fingernails. I think she was going for my eyes, but I held her off and managed to throw her bodily away from me. She fell and hit her head on the table.'

'So she was dead.'

'No, she was knocked out. I went over and knelt down beside her. I found her pulse and it was still beating. She was very pale and out cold but she was still alive. Then as I knelt there on the floor something or someone hit me on the back of the head and I blacked out.'

'Someone hit you? Someone else was there?'

'Must have been but I don't know who and I couldn't prove that there'd been anyone even at the trial.'

'Wasn't there any evidence of anyone else having been in the flat?'

'Plenty to show other people had

been there at other times but nothing to pinpoint that particular evening.'

'And you didn't notice anything?'

Simon shook his head.

'I saw nothing; the only thing I remembered apart from my actual confrontation with Jane was that the room reeked of tobacco, and she didn't smoke. Jane I mean.'

'What happened then?'

'When I came round I found I was lying on the floor with one hell of a headache. Jane was there, too, but in a different place. She was on the other side of the room and her head was smashed against the stone corner of the fireplace. I crawled over to her and felt for her pulse, but this time there was none.'

'Oh, my God!'

'I found the phone and called for the police and an ambulance, and while I waited for them I tried to give Jane the kiss of life.'

He laughed then, without humour, an awful sound to Tara's ear and said,

'The kiss of life! Imagine! She was the kiss of death to me. Anyway, it was obviously no good. Then I began to notice something else. The whole room was a shambles, table and chairs upset, broken glasses, wine spilt, cushions on the floor as though there had been an almighty fight. We hadn't caused that damage, but nothing I could say would convince the police of that.'

'So they arrested you for killing her when you'd done all you could to save her life. Surely they realised you'd hardly have called for them to come if you had done it. I mean you'd have slipped away into the night and left someone else to find her.'

'That came up in my defence, of course,' said Simon, 'but they decided I had killed her by accident during a marital fight and then had been filled with remorse and tried to save her. The court accepted that it was not cold-blooded murder but they could not believe I had not done it by accident, so

I was sent down for manslaughter. The final laugh for Jane if she did but know it.'

He sounded weary and said no more. The silence drifted round them as they sat among the dunes, this time enclosing rather than separating them. The wind whispered through the dry grasses, but neither Tara nor Simon spoke. Night had crept in from the sea, and back along the beach the garish lights of Silverstrand were softened to a glow by the distance.

It was a long silence. There seemed no more to be said and yet there were so many questions between them to be asked and answered. The happiness which had touched Tara the previous evening had drained away and she, too, was left with the shadow of Jane Hamilton across her life. Simon's words echoed in her mind. The evil of Jane affected the lives of everyone who knew her and Tara added silently, and even some who didn't.

At last Simon gently disengaged his

hand, which Tara, unnoticing, was still grasping.

'You'll get cold,' he said. 'Come on, let's go back.'

He got to his feet, and stiffly Tara did the same. She found she had no question in her mind that Simon had told her the truth. She accepted what he said because it was too awful a story to have made up; because Simon was not the man to reveal such degradation as Jane had caused him, lightly or easily. There was so much Tara did not know about Simon but she was utterly convinced that he did not kill Jane. All the time he had been speaking, so softly, so calmly, she had been increasingly aware of the lonely torment he was recalling and she found herself aching to help his banish it from his mind, to convince him he was no longer alone. Very deliberately Tara took both his hands and turning him to face her in the gathering darkness she said, 'Simon, kiss me.'

There was a sudden stillness between

them. Tara could not see his expression but she felt his whole body stiffen. Gently she released his hands and slipping her arms round his neck reached up and pressed her cheek to his.

'Tara?' he said huskily. 'Tara?' And as he felt her arms tighten his own closed convulsively round her and he buried his face in her hair.

'Simon.' Her voice was no more than a whisper. And so he kissed her, her lips, her eyes, her cheeks, her hair, her lips again with all the hunger which had been missing the night before; and Tara, overwhelmed by his longing, returned his kisses with aching happiness.

At length, still holding her close, Simon drew her down into the sandy hollow on the edge of the dunes where they had been sitting before and sheltered by the sandhills and the whispering grasses he began to kiss her again.

9

The moon crept over the horizon, a
luminous disc in the night sky and in its
faint glow Tara could see Simon's face
at last. She was lying on the dry sand
and Simon, propped up on one elbow
was beside her, gazing down at her. He
traced her features with a finger and
smiled as she smiled up at him.

'Simon?'

'Mmmm?' He lifted a strand of her
hair and kissed it. Passion had left him
for a while, but Tara knew it was not far
beneath the tenderness which had
replaced it. Indeed it was there in both
of them. Tara had been a little
frightened by her response to his loving;
his kisses and his gentle exploration of
her body had made her come alive as
she never had before. She knew it was
now her decision. If she reached for
him again the last vestiges of their

control would vanish and though he would not be the first man she had made love with, she knew in her heart there would be no one but Simon from now, and suddenly she wanted to wait. The moment would be too precious to waste, to squander lightly among the sand dunes. She sat up and said teasingly, 'That was a little different from last night.'

'Last night? Last night I hardly dare touch you.'

'You were rather more reserved,' agreed Tara with a grin. 'Polite, perhaps is the word.'

Simon moved to sit beside her, slipping an arm round her as if he were afraid she might disappear.

'Last night I was still Steven Harris to you.' Simon spoke seriously. 'I couldn't say anything until you knew who I really was. I tried a sort of compromise, but it didn't work, did it? You knew there was something wrong. I shouldn't have touched you at all before you knew the truth, but I needed you.'

As he confessed his need his arm tightened round her so that Tara hastened to say, 'You should have told me.'

'Should I? What would you have done? You were all so afraid of me. You, Paul, Mrs Ward . . . What would you have done, Tara?'

Tara sighed. 'I don't know. Kept as far away as possible, I suppose.'

'Perhaps you still should, until I've sorted out my life again,' said Simon. 'Unless of course this is a casual affair as far as you're concerned.' The weary bitterness returned to his voice. Tara caught his mood and said in a small voice, 'Simon, don't. I don't go in for casual affairs much. I'm not very good at them.' She went on with more determination, 'I know how I feel, but what about you? Let's face it, you've been in prison for four years; perhaps almost any woman would do for you. It needn't necessarily be me. It's just that I'm here and . . . ' her voice trailed away and she turned her head from him so that the moonlight should not reveal the tears in her eyes.

Simon released her from his arms and drawing apart from her, said quietly, 'You're right. Four years is a long time, but I can wait. If I'd just wanted to use you as a woman, I'd have tried as Steven Harris last night or sooner. But I know from bitter experience that all good relationships must be founded on honesty and truth, and I wanted so much for us.' He laughed ruefully. 'In some ways you were better off with Steven. He didn't have all the problems that I do.'

Tara reached for his hand and holding it against her cheek said softly, 'But I don't want Steven. It's Simon I want.'

The silence that fell between them said more than any words and they moved quietly into each others arms.

'Now,' said Tara briskly a moment or two later, 'let's begin to get you sorted out. What about Paul?'

'Legally he's mine. I'm his legal

guardian and unless there's a court order against me, there's nothing to stop me taking him away with me. But obviously I can't just uproot him and carry him off. It's clear he's been brought up to hate me, and he's had enough trouble in his short life without my adding to it in that way.'

'But it isn't you he hates,' said Tara, considering. 'He hates the man who has been presented to him as his wicked father. He thought you were marvellous when he thought you were Steven.'

'But I'm not Steven, and he knows it now. When I came to Old Court I wasn't going to pose as anyone but myself, how could I? Mrs Ward would have recognised me at once, even though Paul wouldn't have.'

'But Mrs Ward wasn't there,' said Tara slowly.

'Exactly. When Paul told me she was in hospital, I suddenly realised it meant I was entirely unknown. I could approach him as a stranger and begin to build up something between us; win his confidence, his affection. I hoped that before I had to reveal who I really was, I could have forged such a strong link between us that when he did learn the truth we could overcome his fear and resentment.'

'You were doing well, too,' said Tara. 'He thought the world of you.'

'Until Harper turned up and ruined it all. What did he come down to Silverstrand for?'

'He came because he'd written to Mrs Ward about your release and had had no reply. He wanted to be sure she was prepared. Don't forget he's her solicitor.'

'I know. That's what I'm worried about.'

'Why? What can they do?'

'Well, he can advise her on how to keep Paul. I mean I suppose they can apply to the court and say I'm not a fit person to have care of my son.'

'Because you're supposed to have killed his mother?'

'Exactly. Hardly a recommendation, is it?'

'But you've paid for it!' exclaimed Tara.

'Paid my debt to society? That old cliché? I doubt if that would help much in this case. The needs of the child will be considered as paramount and they'll probably return him to the stability of his grandmother's house, the place he's always been.'

'But his grandmother isn't there now,' pointed out Tara. 'She's ill in hospital and may never get better. She may never be well enough to have charge of a small boy. Particularly as he has a father willing and able to do so himself.'

'I still think she'll fight; or rather Andrew Harper will fight for her.'

The night breeze had stiffened and Tara shivered as it began to stir the sand around them.

'You're cold,' said Simon. 'Come on let's go somewhere warmer.' He pulled her to her feet and they scrambled back down on to the smooth sand of the beach. Arm in arm they strolled slowly towards the bright lights of Silverstrand.

'Couldn't you get in first?' asked Tara suddenly. 'Couldn't you get a court order or something to say that Paul is your son and his grandmother had no right to keep him from you?'

Simon considered this. 'I might, I suppose. But it would probably all come back to my suitability as a father and Jane's death would soon be used against me again.' He laughed bitterly. 'You see what I meant about being trapped by her wickedness. Even now, years after she's dead, she's still able to keep Paul from me and cause me pain. How she would have enjoyed all this.'

'But why did she hate you so much? Why did she want to hurt you?' Tara asked.

'It wasn't just me. She enjoyed hurting anyone. It was simply that I was so much more vulnerable because I loved her. It's easy to hurt someone who loves you.'

'But why did she marry you in the first place?'

'God only knows!' replied Simon with feeling.

A church clock was striking eleven as they climbed the steps from the beach to the promenade. The pubs were closing and their patrons were wandering cheerfully home or moving on to the discos and other night spots; the amplified voice of a caller from a bingo hall announced, 'Eyes down for the final full house this evening, ladies and gentlemen.' Simon and Tara paused at the top of the steps, overcome by the sudden rush of noisy people and the flashing of neon signs.

'Are you hungry?' Simon asked.

Tara, surprised, discovered she was, starving. 'I didn't have any supper myself. I didn't feel like eating.'

'Let's find somewhere then. Several places stay open late round her.'

They found a quiet table in the

corner of an Italian bistro and Simon ordered them lasagna and a bottle of chianti. While they waited for it to come, Tara said, 'Well if the worst comes to the worst what are you going to do? How will you prove to the court that you are a suitable person to look after Paul?'

'Well, to be able to provide him with a suitable home must be the first step; and make it clear that there was someone about to look after him in the holidays and after school. There's a flat over the shop. I used to use it for storage space, but I can soon clean it up and furnish it. It wouldn't be too bad and I'd be downstairs in the shop when Paul came in from school and things.'

'What about your old house?'

'It was in Jane's name. It was part of the price for Paul. When she was killed it was sold and the money put in trust for Paul. It was all in her will. Her executors carried it out.'

'Don't tell me; her executor was . . . ?'

'Andrew Harper.'

136

'What about the trust? Can the money be touched?'

'With the permission of the trustees.'

'Who are?'

'Andrew Harper and Mrs Ward. I strongly suspect it was Paul's trust money that bought Old Court, but I haven't had a chance to find out for certain yet.'

Their meal came and as they were eating Tara came up with another idea.

'If you re-married it would mean you could offer Paul a more stable background. That might well count in your favour.'

'It might,' conceded Simon cautiously.

'We could, you know,' said Tara.

Simon set aside his glass of wine and reached across the table to her.

'It wouldn't be a very good reason for getting married,' he said firmly.

'No,' agreed Tara, 'not if it was the only one.'

Simon's eyes caressed her and she felt the colour flood her face. 'Darling

Tara, if we get married it will have nothing to do with Paul's future, except incidentally. If we get married it will be because we can't live without each other, and not for any other reason.'

Tara, anxious now to change the subject, said with studied cheerfulness, 'Then you'll just have to prove your innocence. You didn't kill Jane, so there is absolutely no reason why you should not have the care of your son. All we have to do is prove it.'

'Exactly!'

'What?' Tara had not really been serious in her comment, but Simon obviously was.

'That's exactly what I'd decided myself. When I was under arrest for killing Jane, I couldn't do any investigating myself of course, but I'm sure there's evidence somewhere that the police didn't find.'

'Evidence? What sort of thing?'

'Well, for a start, Jane's records.'

'Records?' Tara was puzzled.

'Do you remember I told you Jane

said she kept a record of all her affairs? She said each person had a record card. Well, peculiar as the actual idea may be, I think she was probably telling the truth. It would have been just like her. Anyhow, they were never found. I told the police about them of course, but when they didn't come to light it was generally agreed that she had made it up and just said it to taunt me.' Simon smiled wryly. 'They didn't know Jane like I knew her. I don't think they looked very hard, and of course Mrs Ward was no help. She accused me of trying to smear Jane's reputation, when the poor girl was no longer able to defend herself against me.'

'But what help would these record cards be if you did find them?'

'I'm not sure; perhaps we could learn the names of some of the other people who she was involved with. Someone else who had a motive to kill her might emerge. It would certainly prove that she was not the innocent angel everyone thought.'

'Did everyone think so?'

'Well, certain things came out at the trial which suggested she was not, but there was nothing conclusive.'

'What kind of thing?' asked Tara. She pushed aside her plate and leant forward, her elbows resting on the table, her chin cupped in her hands.

'The main one was the secret mirror. They found one of the mirrors set into the bedroom wall was not only a mirror, but could be used as a window for spying from the living room; so that you could see into the bedroom without being seen.'

'I see,' breathed Tara. 'Didn't the police think that was strange?'

'Of course; and there were several other mirrors in the bedroom, one in the ceiling above the bed. But there's no law against it and it wasn't Jane who was on trial.'

'But surely it proved that, well, that she was a call girl of some sort.'

'It indicated it, but that was considered irrelevant in what was regarded as a purely domestic killing. This wasn't a major murder trial, conducted in a blaze of publicity, and domestic killings are happening all the time. They decided that I must have killed her under extreme provocation, having discovered what she was doing.'

'Did you know the mirror was there?' asked Tara. 'When you were in the room with her could you see into the bedroom?'

'No, I had no idea. She had a huge modern painting on one wall, it was discovered behind that.'

'Was there anything else?'

'Some unusual items of clothing in the wardrobe, but nothing that couldn't be explained given a little imagination.'

'But no record cards or notebooks.'

'None. Do you want a pud?'

Tara shook her head. 'A coffee would be nice.'

Simon ordered coffee and brandy for each of them and when the waiter had brought it, Tara asked, 'Where else might the records be, if not in her flat?'

'I don't know, but I thought the first place to look must be in her mother's house.'

'You think her mother might have them?'

'She might.'

'But surely she'd have handed them over when the police were looking for them.'

'Would *you*? If you thought you had something that would damn your daughter's name for ever, something that would prove she was a common whore? If Mrs Ward did have those records there was no way she was going to hand them over and perhaps have them read out in court.'

'But they might have saved you,' cried Tara.

'There was no doubt in Mrs Ward's mind that I had killed Jane. Anything she had which might discredit Jane would not alter that fact in her opinion. She was convinced I had killed her and no muck-raking of her daughter's reputation could justify that. She may not even know what she's got. They're probably locked away, in a briefcase or a tin like a cash box or deed box, something like that.'

'She must know what's in it if there is such a thing. She must at least have looked.'

'Perhaps she didn't want to know. Perhaps she suspected what Jane was, but didn't want to have it proved. I mean, she always pretended not to know there was anything wrong between Jane and me; she just couldn't accept it.'

'I still think she knows what she's got, if she's got it,' said Tara firmly. 'She may not have studied it, but she must have looked if only to be sure it wasn't something vitally important.' A devastating thought struck Tara. 'But suppose she's destroyed them. Suppose she did have them and read them and burned them all, so Jane's reputation should be preserved for ever?'

Simon looked weary. 'Don't think I haven't thought of that,' he said. 'It's really the most likely theory, but I have to look, to make sure, and until I know they've been destroyed I live on hope. Mrs Ward idolised Jane, so she may have kept everything. Anyway, I'm sure Old Court is the place to start looking,' Simon went on. 'Do you know if there's a safe anywhere? I couldn't find one.'

Tara glanced at him in surprise. 'Have you been searching already?'

'Of course,' replied Simon. 'I couldn't waste the chance of looking while I was still unrecognised.' He grinned ruefully. 'There'd be little opportunity afterwards. I'm sorry I frightened you that time.'

'Frightened me?' Tara was puzzled, and then her brow cleared as light dawned and she realised what he meant.

'You! Simon Hamilton, it was you poking about in Mrs Ward's cupboard the other night. There wasn't an intruder at all!'

'No, I'm afraid there wasn't. I got the shock of my life when you sat up in bed, I can tell you. I thought you were safely asleep downstairs.' Simon laughed. 'Nearly frightened me to death you did. I hadn't even glanced at the bed. I just knew no one was there.'

'I frightened you to death!' cried Tara indignantly. 'What do you think you did to me! I thought you were Paul's father and — '

'And so I am!' They both laughed at that.

'But where did you go?'

'Down the drainpipe, as you thought, but in at my own window below, not out through the courtyard.'

'The gate was open.'

'By chance. I had to throw my clothes off and leap into bed so that I could be ready to emerge when you gave the alarm. The first time you knocked I was still getting undressed.'

Tara had a sudden vision of Simon tossing clothes round the bedroom and making a dive for his bed as she knocked at the door; she began to laugh and once she had started she found she could not stop. The laughter welled up inside her, bubbling with delight as it escaped and infected Simon, so that for a moment the sound of their mirth caused other diners to turn their heads. In that instant Tara saw Simon as he could be; his worries momentarily forgotten, his face creased with laughter, happiness shining in his eyes and she knew then that she would do everything in her power to help him achieve his aim, to establish his innocence and regain the care of his son, so that such happiness should not be fleeting, but would be with him always.

10

The day had lasted for ever, the morning when Tara had been asked to visit Mrs Ward could have been weeks ago. In the small space of a day, less than twenty-four hours in fact, the whole world had changed; her life had entirely new purpose and direction and the woman who returned to the grey stone guest house long after midnight was subtly but irrevocably different from the one who had called at the hospital that morning or slipped out through the garden gate to meet a killer in the evening.

Old Court was in semi-darkness with only a nightlight burning on each landing when Tara let herself in at last and crept up to her room. Afraid Andrew might be waiting up for her she had said goodnight to Simon in the deep shadow of a plane tree at the end of the road. For a moment they clung together, each drawing strength from the other and then with a final kiss they parted, their plans made and a meeting arranged for the next evening.

An absolute silence enveloped the house as if the whole place were holding its breath, poised, waiting for something to happen. As she reached the top of the first staircase, Tara wondered if she should look in on Paul, but decided against it; his door was probably still locked and there was no point in waking him up just to see how he was.

Lying in the quiet darkness of her room, Tara relived her eventful evening; her heart turned over at the memory of his kisses and as she recalled the expression in Simon's eyes as he had looked down at her she felt light-headed. However, with great determination she forced herself to forget her quivering senses and concentrated her mind on their plan to try and establish Simon's innocence. The first thing to do was to take up the search Simon had begun, to try and find the records Jane had kept.

'I didn't get a chance to hunt through Mrs Ward's cupboard before you woke up,' Simon had said. 'it's a big one which runs along under the eaves and there are all sorts of cases and boxes stacked at the side. It'll take a fair time to go through them all.'

'Our main problem is going to be Andrew Harper,' said Tara thoughtfully. 'He's moved into Mrs Ward's room. I'll have to begin looking while I know he's safely at the hospital.'

They had agreed on that, but now Tara, pondering their plan in the darkness, had a better idea. There was no one in the room Simon had been occupying, so she would get Andrew to move down there, then she could go secretly and lock herself into Mrs Ward's room without fear of his walking in and catching her there. With this decision taken, Tara allowed herself the luxury of imagining herself again in Simon's arms and drifted at last into a deep and blissful sleep.

The shrill of the alarm startled her awake next morning and Tara dragged herself from sleep to begin the day. There was nothing she could do to advance their cause until after breakfast and so she relegated Simon to the back of her mind and turned her attention to the guests. Andrew came down with the others and lingered in the dining room over an extra cup of coffee, his newspaper propped up in front of him. When Tara came in to clear the tables he said, 'How's Paul now? Better this morning?'

'He hasn't come down yet,' replied Tara, pausing in the doorway with the tray. 'I thought I'd let him sleep on. It'll do him good.'

'Well, when he comes down let me know. I'll be in the lounge.'

Tara returned to the table next to his and setting down the tray said, 'I was thinking, why don't you move down into the room Simon Hamilton had? There's no one booked for it.'

Andrew looked up in mild surprise. 'Why should I?'

'Well . . . ' Tara felt suddenly awkward as if her motive for wanting him to move were written clearly on her face, 'well, I just thought that perhaps you'd be happier there, not crammed in with all Mrs Ward's things. I mean, well it is her own bedroom, not one of the guestrooms. She might not like you there,' Tara finished feebly as she met with the stonewall of his rejection.

'I'm perfectly comfortable where I am,' Andrew said lightly. 'Mrs Ward won't mind in the least; and it gives you an extra room if someone should arrive unexpectedly.'

'But don't you think — ' began Tara.

'I have no intention of changing rooms, Tara. I shall stay where I am, in the room next to Paul.' He spoke with finality and turned back to his newspaper. With a shrug Tara picked up the tray again and went out to the kitchen. Once there she left the dirty crockery on the draining board, poured herself a cup of coffee and sat down to think again. She was aware of an entirely different attitude from Andrew this morning; he had spoken to her as an employer to an employee. Probably because she had demanded extra help the night before, laying down her terms, saying exactly what she was and was not prepared to do. She had made it clear that her job was the guest house and the guest house alone with no commitment to the family at all, so she could hardly complain if Andrew now treated her strictly within those terms. Or, the terrible thought nagged her, did Andrew know she had met Simon last night? Did he realise that she was as good as a spy in the camp? How could he know? Surely he had not followed her. Tara dismissed the idea as too ridiculous to be given serious consideration, but the coolness in his tone had been unmistakable. Perhaps he guessed rather than knew where she had been. If so he would not trust her with Paul again, he would take sole responsibility for the child himself. Tara was not at all sure that this was a good idea. Simon had impressed upon her that she was his only link with Paul.

'He'll be feeling very alone and probably frightened,' Simon had said. 'Look after him for me, Tara. He needs someone to hang on to until he's come to terms with everything.'

She had promised to do so, but with Andrew hostile, or at least remote, it might not be as easy as it had seemed.

Mrs Vernon, who came in for an hour on Sundays in the high season, pottered into the kitchen and stared round at the debris of breakfast.

'Bit behind 'and are you, dearie?' she remarked.

Tara managed a smile. 'Just a bit, Mrs Vernon. I suppose you couldn't stack the dishwasher for me, could you?'

'Me, dearie? I don't do dishes.' Mrs Vernon sounded faintly apologetic, but firm.

'No, of course not. Perhaps the beds . . . ?'

'Not beds, dearie. Cleaning. I'll do the dining room first, shall I? Give you a chance to catch up.'

Afraid of upsetting the old lady and losing her, Tara nodded and thanked her. Mrs Vernon collected the dusters and vacuum cleaner and wandered off in the direction of the dining room. Before Mrs Vernon could complain that that was not ready for her attentions either, Tara slipped quietly upstairs and tried Paul's bedroom door. It was still locked.

'Paul!' she called softly. 'Paul? It's me — Tara. I've come to see if you want some breakfast.'

There was no reply. Silence emanated from the room, a complete silence; no scuffling or movement of any kind; no coughing or crying as there had been last night. On impulse Tara knelt down and put her eye to the keyhole. The key had been removed and she was able to see a limited portion of the room, which included part of the bed and the bedside table.

The quilt on the bed was rumpled and the pillow was askew, but there was no sign of Paul. Tara put her lips to the keyhole and called again, but still there was no reply.

Suddenly certain that the child was no longer in the room, Tara banged loudly on the door, rattling the handle in frustration at her inability to get in. Then turning, she hurried downstairs to the lounge to find Andrew, still buried complacently in his paper. He glanced up as Tara burst into the room. 'Now what's the matter?' he drawled as he read the anxiety in her face.

'Paul's gone. He's not in his room, I'm sure.'

'Gone!' Andrew's complacency vanished as he leapt to his feet. 'Gone where?'

'I don't know,' snapped Tara. 'I'm certain his room's empty, but the door's locked.'

Andrew took the stairs three at a time and reaching Paul's room tried the door, rattling the handle angrily. Then he, too, crouched down and peered through the keyhole.

'Have you got a spare key?' he demanded, turning to Tara.

'Probably,' answered Tara, already on her way to look, 'there're certainly spares to all the guestrooms downstairs.'

The spare key board hung in a cupboard in the kitchen. All the keys were labelled with room numbers except two; these she grabbed and racing back upstairs handed them to Andrew. The first fitted into the keyhole but did not turn the lock, the second operated the lock smoothly and in an instant Andrew had the door open and they stepped into the room.

Paul was not there. Though the bed was rumpled, Tara decided it had been lain on rather than slept in, and investigating further she discovered Paul's pyjamas were not there, nor was his teddy bear, still so necessary at bedtime. His toothbrush had gone from his toothglass on the basin and his anorak was missing from the hook on the back of the door. She pointed these things out to Andrew who was peering out of the window as if he expected to see Paul slipping away through the garden door.

'Other things have probably gone, too,' went on Tara, 'I don't know what else to look for.' She looked round the room again and then added, 'His Nottingham Forest bag. It was always hanging on the back of his chair.'

'Bastard Hamilton must have come for him,' snarled Andrew, glaring at her. 'Once he'd been recognised it was the only thing he could do.'

Knowing that Simon had not been near the child, but unable to prove it without saying how she knew, made Tara pause.

'I should have thought that rather unlikely,' she said slowly. 'It's far more probable that he's simply run away, don't you think? There was no one here he knew well enough to confide in. Neither of us was close enough to comfort him. It was all too much and he's run away.'

'Run away? Where would he run to?'

Tara shrugged. 'Did he have any particular friends? Another family he could use as a haven?'

'How do I know?' snapped Andrew pacing the room. 'I don't know who his friends are.'

'No godparents or anything?'

'Godparents!' Andrew gave a bark of laughter. 'Jane didn't go in for that sort of thing.'

'I'll try the school, then,' said Tara briskly. 'They should be able to give me a list of his friends.'

'Will anyone be there?' said Andrew a little more calmly. 'It's still holidays, isn't it? And Sunday at that.'

'I can but try,' answered Tara. 'You try the hospital.'

'The hospital?' For a moment Andrew seemed at a loss.

'Mrs Ward. She's his only link with stability, perhaps he's gone to find her. If not she may have some idea as to where he might go.'

Andrew nodded and strode downstairs to begin the search.

'If we've not found him by lunchtime we'll have to call in the police,' he called over his shoulder. 'I'm going to the hospital now. Ring me there if he turns up.'

Left alone Tara's first instinct was to let Simon know Paul was missing, but, as she realised with a jolt, he had said he had got a room but he had not said where. It could be anywhere. She had no way of contacting him. So, praying Simon would telephone her during the day, Tara turned her attention to finding Paul. She had said she would work through the school and so she set out to do so.

She knew none of Paul's friends; he had never brought anyone home with him since she had been at Old Court, neither had he been out to play with anyone else. She knew where his school was though because Paul had pointed it out on one of their walks through the town. Remembering there was a board outside Tara hurried round to the school. It was closed as she expected, but she was able to make a note of the telephone numbers of both the head-master and the school caretaker, which were displayed on the board. Hurrying home again she dialled the head's number. It rang and rang, but Tara finally had to accept that there was no reply. She tried again immediately in case she had misdialled, but the ringing tone went on and on until at last she admitted defeat. Then she tried the caretaker and eventually had to give up when it was clear there was no one there either.

Tara flopped into a chair and wondered what to do next. Short of wandering the streets of Silverstrand on the off chance of seeing Paul, there seemed little more she could do until Andrew came back. Perhaps the boy had not run away at all, perhaps he had just gone out for a walk; to get away from them all; to give himself a chance to adjust to the new knowledge he had of his father. But Tara's mind kept coming back to the Nottingham Forest bag and the other things she had noticed missing from his bedroom, and she knew in her heart that Paul had tried to escape from them all.

Mrs Vernon appeared once again in the kitchen and casting a disapproving glance at the breakfast things still stacked on the draining board, sniffed and said, 'I'm off now, miss. See yer termorrer.'

Tara, well aware of the disapproval, said wearily, 'You haven't seen Paul, have you, Mrs Vernon? He's missing.'

Mrs Vernon softened a little and said, 'Gorn off without saying, 'as 'e? Little tike! No, I 'aven't seen 'im. P'raps 'e's round 'is mate's 'ouse, y'know that kid David Castle, lives in Dunes Crescent.'

'David Castle! Of course, that was the name of the boy he met the other day. Oh, thank you, Mrs Vernon, you're fantastic.' Tara reached for the telephone directory and turned up Castle.

Mrs Vernon smiled and said, ''Ope you find 'im, dearie. I'll keep an eye open as I go 'ome and send 'im back quick if I see 'im.'

'Thank you very much, Mrs Vernon, see you tomorrow.' Tara went back to the telephone and dialling the number she had found in the book waited anxiously for a reply, but yet again the ringing remained unanswered. With nothing more for her to do, Tara gave her attention to the kitchen and set about clearing it up and preparing lunch. It was far too late to roast the joint of beef expected by the guests on a Sunday, they would just have to have it for supper. They could manage with cold meat and salad as they did on a week day.

As she was peeling the potatoes the doorbell rang and Tara, wiping her hands on her apron, went to see who it was. There, beaming on the doorstep, was Mandy from the agency.

Tara cried out in delight, 'Oh, Mandy, thank goodness. Everything's beginning to get on top of me.'

Mandy laughed and said, 'You do look a bit shattered. Never fear, Mandy's here. Just tell me what's to be done.'

11

Mandy was as good as her word and within minutes she was back in the kitchen with Tara, washing lettuce, chopping tomatoes and slicing cucumber.

'Now then,' she said, 'tell me what's going on. Derek at the agency said you sounded desperate.'

So as they worked companionably together Tara gave Mandy an edited version of the situation at Old Court; explaining about Mrs Ward's stroke, about Simon and Paul, about Andrew Harper; but carefully leaving out her own relationship with Simon, the truth about Jane and the plans afoot for trying to establish Simon's innocence.

'So Andrew is at the hospital to see if Paul tried to go to his grandmother, and if he didn't Andrew'll ask Mrs Ward if she can think of anywhere he might go.'

'That won't help her recovery,' remarked Mandy, measuring out oil and vinegar to make a vinaigrette for the tomatoes. 'She'll be worried stiff about Paul if your friend Andrew tells her he's missing.'

'I know,' Tara was troubled, 'but what else can we do? If Paul's not home by lunchtime we're going to call the police.'

'Perhaps Paul has gone off with that father of his,' suggested Mandy. 'I mean, he is his father after all.'

'I doubt it,' said Tara, electing not to tell Mandy the true reason why. 'He's been brought up to hate his father. I doubt if he'd run to him. Away from him more likely.' Which is sadly true, Tara thought to herself.

'Hmmm. I see. Well, I think you're right, the police will have to be told. Now, what do we give the customers for pud?'

Andrew arrived back as the girls finished laying up the tables for lunch. He greeted Mandy absentmindedly and then said, 'He's not been near the hospital as far as I can discover.'

'What did Mrs Ward say? Was she very upset?'

'She was asleep. They wouldn't let me wake her up and when I explained how urgent it was they were even more adamant; said that she wasn't to be worried.'

'Perhaps we should phone the police now and report him missing,' suggested Tara. 'They've far more resources than we have. I mean they can check the station to see if anyone saw him catch a train, and watch the roads for him.'

'Did he have any money?' asked Mandy suddenly. Tara glanced up at the kitchen mantelpiece where Paul's elephant money box had stood. It, too, was missing.

'He's taken his money box,' she said. 'It was here on the mantelpiece.'

'Then he could be anywhere,' sighed Andrew. 'How much was in it, do you know?'

Tara shrugged. 'It was fairly heavy,

but it could all have been pennies.'

The telephone shrilled beside her, and Tara snatched the receiver in the sudden hope it would be news of Paul.

'Old Court Guest House. Hallo.'

'Tara, it's me.' Simon spoke softly, but immediately Tara stiffened; Andrew was standing less than a yard from her.

'Good morning,' she said politely. 'Can I help you?'

'You sound as if someone's with you.'

'That's right.'

'Is it Harper?'

'Yes, but I'm afraid we're fully booked just now.'

'Any news?'

'Well, of course we're always busy at this time of year.'

'Can we meet as arranged?'

'Thank you for the enquiry. I'm sorry we can't help, perhaps later on?'

'If you can't get there this evening, I'll be there again tomorrow.'

'Fine, we may hear from you then. Thank you for calling. Goodbye.'

'Message received and understood.

Goodbye, my darling.'

Tara replaced the receiver and felt her heart pounding. She took a deep breath before she turned to face Andrew and Mandy again.

'Who was that?' asked Andrew.

'Oh, just a family looking for somewhere to stay,' replied Tara and without pause went on, 'Are you going to phone the police, Andrew? I really do think we should.'

When the police arrived it was lunchtime. Tara and Mandy were occupied with the guests so Andrew took the constable into the lounge. Within minutes however, he called down to Tara and she had to leave Mandy to cope on her own and join the two men.

'Now, Miss Dereham,' said the policeman, 'Mr Harper has explained it all to me. He's very concerned that the boy's father may have kidnapped him. I understand he was here before.'

'He was,' admitted Tara, 'but none of us knew he was Paul's father. He registered in a different name.'

'I see. Do you think that it's probable the child has gone to his father?'

Once again Tara gave her reasons for thinking it unlikely. She felt extremely uncomfortable about it all as she spoke. Part of her wanted to confide the whole story to the police, but the other half knew that to do so could well jeopardize Simon's chances of claiming custody of Paul. Carefully she told only the truth, but equally carefully left out any references to her meeting with Simon the previous evening. The policeman listened intently and then moved on to the safer ground of Paul's description, the clothes he was wearing and the things he had taken.

All the time Tara was aware of Andrew's eyes upon her; boring into her as if he were able to read her thoughts, as if he suspected that she knew more than she said. She was afraid he would confront her with evidence of her duplicity and as soon as she was able she reminded them she

169

was needed downstairs and escaped thankfully to the kitchen. As the policeman was leaving, Andrew put his head round the door and asked Tara whether she knew if there was a recent photograph of Paul anywhere. Without a word she reached for the frame that stood on the kitchen mantelpiece and handed it to Andrew, and armed with this, a school photo, and Tara's description of the boy's clothes, the police left to start the search.

Andrew joined Mandy and Tara in the kitchen to smoke a cigarillo and drink a cup of coffee, while they cleared up the meal.

'The police will check the station. It's unlikely he's got a lift and travelled by road; most people would hesitate to pick up a seven-year-old with a suitcase.'

'Unless of course they're keen on seven-year-olds,' remarked Mandy brightly.

'I wasn't going to point that out,' said Andrew brusquely, stubbing his cigarillo viciously into the saucer of his coffee cup. 'There's no use in getting panicky about that sort of thing until we know something definite.'

'Sorry,' cooed Mandy and returned to the dishes.

That afternoon Tara did not go out. She would not see Simon because their meeting was arranged for the evening, and anyway she wanted to be at Old Court in case there was any news of Paul. Andrew also decided to stay in and plumped himself down in front of the television to watch the cricket. Mandy went out to explore Silver-strand. Tara had hoped Andrew might go out for a while to give her a chance to investigate the boxes in the dormer cupboard under the eaves in Mrs Ward's bedroom, but with him in the house, she dared not. At any moment he might leave the cricket and come upstairs for something. She could so easily be caught and she had no valid reason to offer for poking about in one of Mrs Ward's private cupboards, so she decided to try and eliminate other possible hiding places first. She knew Simon had done the same but it was quite likely he had missed something in his efforts to hunt unnoticed. But Tara had no more luck than he. There was nowhere which could conceal anything like a safe, no locked cupboards or doors, and Tara felt quite certain that Jane's records, if they indeed existed, would be locked away safely, not left where chance might reveal them.

Tara returned to her bedroom. As she passed the lounge she peeped in to see Andrew apparently dozing in front of the television, but though tempted, prudence demanded that she should still make no effort to search his room. No, she would have to wait until he went to the hospital to see Mrs Ward; then at least she could have some idea of the time she had and could insure he did not walk in on her unexpectedly.

She lay on her bed considering what Simon could do if they did manage to find Jane's records. Would it be enough evidence to get the trial re-opened? Where could Paul be? Poor little boy, so confused. She wondered if there was anything else they could be doing to find him. Should she be out searching the beach, or milling with the crowds on the promenade looking; peering anxiously at every child in jeans and a T-shirt? It would mean she was doing something, however small, towards finding him, but she was determined not to leave the guest house. If Paul came home and she was not there she would not be at all surprised if Andrew spirited him away somewhere so that Simon would not be able to find him. Though her thoughts were whirling, Tara drifted into a deep sleep, the troubles of the last two days had taken their toll and she was exhausted; she slept dreamlessly until a sharp rap on her door jerked her awake. It was Mandy home from her walk and wondering about the evening meal.

They were just dishing up the vegetables when the door bell chimed.

Tara went to answer it and found Tom
Gurney, the ferryman, on the step with
Paul, palefaced, at his side. For a
moment she stared at him and then
dropping down beside him, gathered
the child into her arms saying, 'Paul!
Thank God you're safe. Where on earth
have you been? We've been so worried.'

For a moment Paul stood rigid in
Tara's arms, not responding to her
embrace, then just as she was drawing
away, he burst into tears and flung his
arms round her neck. Quickly Tara
picked him up and carried him indoors
followed by the burly Tom Gurney with
Paul's Nottingham Forest bag over his
shoulder.

'Can you cope?' Tara asked Mandy.
'Paul's just come home.'

'Yes, I'm fine,' said Mandy cheerfully,
carving the meat with quick dexterity.

Tara settled Paul into Mrs Ward's
chair and turning to Tom Gurney said,
'Thank you so much for bringing him
home, Tom, we've been so worried.
Where was he?'

'Over at the boatyard,' answered Tom, depositing Paul's bag on the table.

'The boatyard!' cried Tara. 'Why didn't I think of that? But why the luggage?' She turned to Paul again. 'Why did you take your bag, Paul?' The boy did not answer, but cowered lower into the chair.

'Time for questions later, I should think,' said Tom quietly. 'He's hungry, I'll be bound.'

'Are you, Paul? When did you last eat? I'll get something now.'

Tom Gurney moved towards the door and Tara saw the look of desperation as Paul half moved to follow him and then dropped sadly back into the chair.

'Come over and see me again soon, Paul,' said the ferryman gently. Paul said nothing, simply stared after him in despairing silence. Tara went with Tom to the front door.

'What was he doing?' she asked softly. 'Why did he go to the boatyard?'

'As far as I can tell,' replied Tom Gurney solemnly, 'he was running away to sea.'

'He was what?' Tara was incredulous. 'To sea?'

'That's about the size of it. He was caught trying to stow away on a visiting boat — a Frenchie. Unfortunately for him there was nowhere much to hide on a boat that size and they found him before they sailed.' Tom looked speculatively at Tara. 'I don't know what's wrong, miss, but something's up. I never seen a boy in such a state.'

'I know,' agreed Tara. 'He's had a terrible shock and he's awfully confused, but he'll be all right now. I'll look after him.'

Andrew came downstairs for dinner as Tom took his leave and demanded, 'What's going on, Tara? Who was that?'

Tara sighed. 'Paul's in the kitchen. Tom brought him back.'

'He's what?' roared Andrew, making for the kitchen door. 'Why the hell didn't you tell me?' Tara grabbed at

Andrew's arm and said sharply, 'He's only just this minute arrived. Listen, the boy's all in. He's frightened and hungry. You must be gentle with him.'

Andrew jerked his arm away and strode into the kitchen. Paul was still huddled in his grandmother's armchair and on seeing Andrew's angry face, shrank even further, his eyes staring terrified from his tear-stained face.

'Young man, we have the police out looking for you!' thundered Andrew. Tara crossed quickly between them and placing herself firmly in front of Andrew said in a low, scathing voice, 'Then you'd better ring them and tell them he's been found.' Confronted by her barely controlled fury, Andrew turned abruptly and went to the telephone. Tara reached for Paul's hand and pulled him up out of the chair. Picking up the Nottingham Forest bag with her other hand she led the exhausted child up the stairs to his room where she soon had him in bed, the comforting teddy unpacked from

the bag and clutched tightly beside
him.

'Now,' said Tara cheerfully, 'I'll get
you something to eat and then you
can settle down for a good night's
sleep. You can tell us all about it in
the morning.'

She took him supper on a tray, but
before he had finished it his head was
heavy on his pillow, his eyelids droop-
ing. Apart from thanking her in a small
voice for the food he had said nothing;
but as she opened the door to take the
tray downstairs Paul called after her.
She turned back.

'What is it, Paul?'

'You won't go away, will you? Not
tonight. You won't go out tonight and
leave me?' He sounded so vulnerable
that Tara's promise was instantly given.

'No, Paul, I won't. I'll be here all
night, just downstairs.'

'Couldn't you sleep in Gran's room?'

'I can't, darling. Uncle Andrew's in
there. But I'll be in my usual room, not
far, just downstairs. I promise I'll come

if you call. I won't go out.' Simon would definitely have to wait until tomorrow. 'Go to sleep now, like a good boy and we'll sort things out in the morning.'

12

The next day was sparkling diamond bright. When Tara threw back her curtains and the dazzling morning light streamed into her bedroom, she had the feeling that this was a day of great importance and her heart beat faster with an inexplicable excitement and expectation. For a moment she watched two butterflies cavorting in the sunshine, fluttering brilliance in the summer air; a black cat stretched languidly on the garden wall, unrolling its body to the increasing warmth of the sun. It was an instant of tranquility to strengthen her before she must return regretfully to the reality of the day, and that reality was to be harsh enough when it came.

Andrew was down early, ready for breakfast before the guests.

'Wake that boy,' he told Tara. 'I've got to go to London. I'll take him with me.

I'm not prepared to leave him on his own down here.'

'Why ever not?' demanded Tara hotly. 'Nothing'll happen to him here. Anyway, he won't be on his own. I'll be here.'

'Maybe, but I've no doubt his father isn't far away and I'm not going to risk him carrying off the boy while I'm in London.'

'So you're going to carry him off yourself.'

'Don't be ridiculous, Tara. We shall be back this evening, but if I'm going to leave my office to run itself for a few days, I have to go in today and sort a few things out.'

It sounded reasonable enough; after all when he had come down to Silverstrand on Saturday he had not expected to stay more than one night. It was Mrs Ward's illness which had changed his plans. Tara felt torn by Andrew's suggestion. She was loath to let Paul disappear with him, but she did not see how she could prevent it. She had no authority over Paul. She was worried about him though. How would he be after the painful events of the weekend? He was probably still very upset. Perhaps in a way it might be better for Paul to have the excitement of a trip to London than to sit around moping at Old Court. Anyway, Tara realised, it would give her a marvellous opportunity to search the dormer cupboard. She had been despairing of the chance, for she knew Andrew would not leave Paul while there was any chance Simon might try to see him and entice him away if not worse; but if they were both safely in London there was little danger that she would be interrupted in her task.

Tara went to wake Paul and found him reading in bed, still pale and looking miserable, but when he heard Andrew proposed to take him up to London, his face was transformed and he jumped out of bed with a shout.

'London! Can I go, Tara? Can I go?'

Tara, in no position to refuse him

anyway, agreed that he could and as if the flood gates had been unlocked, he began to talk, words cascaded from him without pause for answer and by the time he had dressed and breakfasted, Tara knew all the events of the day before. The only person he did not mention, either directly or by implication, was his father. It was as if Simon had ceased to exist for the child, and for the moment Tara was content that it should be so.

After breakfast Tara waved Andrew and Paul goodbye, and spent most of the morning working along side Mandy and Mrs Vernon. Mrs Vernon disappeared at noon and having served lunch to only one couple, Tara pleaded a headache and said she would lie down.

'It's the heat, I expect,' she told Mandy. 'I find it gets to me if I'm tired.'

Mandy sympathised, but was determined to make the most of the afternoon sun.

'I'll be back in time to do the dinner,' she promised. 'I'm just going on the beach for a couple of hours to top up my tan.'

At last Tara was alone in the house. Quickly she ran upstairs to Mrs Ward's room. She intended to make a thorough job of the search as there might not be another opportunity. The bedroom door was shut and when she tried the handle it would not open. The door was locked. Tara stood staring at it stupidly. She had never considered that Andrew might have locked his door before leaving, but now she was faced with the fact that he had, and removed the key.

'Oh, no!' Tara wailed, and beating her fists on the door in frustration she cried out, 'Damn you! Damn you!' The noise she made echoed strangely through the silent house and she stopped abruptly. Suppose one of the guests was, unknown to her, in his room, he would think she had gone mad. She flopped down on to the landing in a wave of despair. Then her eyes rested on Paul's bedroom door standing ajar with its key in its lock. Perhaps it would open either door. Tara leapt to her feet again and wrenching the key from Paul's door, slipped it into the keyhole of Andrew's. It fitted but it would not turn the lock. She withdrew it despondently and was just replacing it when she remembered how they had got into Paul's room the day before. She ran downstairs two at a time and collected the other unlabelled spare key from the board in the kitchen, and was back up the two flights of stairs in a time which would have done credit to a first class athlete.

In a moment she had the door open and paused on the threshold, listening. The house was completely silent. Leaving the door ajar so that she should hear any footsteps on the stairs, she slipped into the room.

Andrew was not a tidy man; there were clothes tossed in a heap on the chair, his bed was supposedly made, the quilt having been dragged across it hurriedly, but it bulged untidily. An ashtray overflowing with butts stood on the table by the bed. The windows were firmly closed and the curtains drawn across. The room was hot and the air rank with the stale smell of his cigarillos. Tara wrinkled her nose, but knowing she must leave everything untouched went straight to the cupboard under the eaves.

It was a deep cupboard, almost a tiny room, with a ceiling which slanted steeply to meet the floor. An unshaded bulb jutted from a socket on the inside wall which, when Tara found the switch, illuminated the whole cupboard. Across the end was a rail of Mrs Ward's clothes, coats and dresses on hangers, and a rack of shoes underneath; and in a neat row along the outside wall where the ceiling met the floor were several cardboard boxes, a trunk and three suitcases.

Quickly Tara peered into the boxes. The first contained books. She lifted the top one out. It was a copy of a rather racy novel, a best-seller in its day, and scrawled in a flamboyant hand was the name *Jane Ward*. The second book was the same and the third. A box of Jane's books; swiftly and methodically Tara unpacked each book, shaking it gently to reveal anything hidden among the pages, flicking through to be certain it was indeed what it purported to be and then laying it aside and turning to the next. She found nothing. It was what it seemed, simply a box of Jane's books. Tara repacked them and began on the second box. This was full of letters, yellowed with age, faded photographs, newspaper cuttings about fashions and changing styles and advertisements for various products in which the model was always the same, blonde and dark-eyed. Jane?

Tara glanced through the letters; they were all addressed to Jane and mostly letters from admirers; a few were from friends, but none gave any clue that Jane was not what she had set herself up to be, a successful model. The photographs were a mixture of holiday snaps obviously taken by an amateur, and professionally posed pictures of Jane at her most glamorous. Tara half-expected to find indecent ones among these, but there were none. The box was a harmless collection of memorabilia.

Tara opened a suitcase next. It was full of clothes; dresses and blouses made of the softest silk, luxurious cashmere jerseys, delicate lace under-wear, negligees, nightdresses frothy with frills, couture evening gowns and cocktail dresses, silk scarves and soft leather gloves. All of them striking in style and design, magnificent in their colour, originality and daring. Jane's clothes folded neatly and packed away; a sweet scent clung to them, a cloying sweetness compounded by layer upon layer of clothing crushed together in the confines of the suitcase. It made Tara recoil. She was more aware of Jane and of what she had been, now that she had discovered her clothes, than at any time since Simon had first mentioned her. Jane's presence pervaded the room, almost overpowering Tara, and hastily trying not to inhale the scent which she felt might never leave her nostrils, she established there was nothing but clothes in the case and repacked it.

One of the other cases proved to be just the same, packed full with beautiful clothes, and the third was empty.

Disinclined to unpack every garment as she had from the first case Tara felt among the clothes in the second case but not surprisingly discovered nothing of further interest. The same cloying sweetness emanated from this suitcase, too, and Tara was relieved to close it quickly.

The third cardboard box was full of old toys, baby toys which Paul had long outgrown, but which for some reason his grandmother had been reluctant to give away. Perhaps they dated from the days before Jane was killed. It was clear that Mrs Ward had destroyed few if any of her daughter's personal possessions. All had been stored with care, as if by keeping her things Mrs Ward was able to keep some part of Jane. The clothes in the suitcases must have cost a fortune, and it was while she was pondering this thought that another idea struck Tara. If Jane had worn clothes like these, she almost certainly had jewellery to match. Obviously that must be in a far safer place than a case in an attic cupboard. The bank perhaps? Or were they hidden away with the most secret of Jane's possessions, the records of her affairs?

Tara turned her attention to the trunk. It was locked. She stared at it angrily. If it was locked it must contain something of value, but she was unwilling to try to break it open, thus leaving evidence of her search; anyhow she had nothing with which to lever the clasps. As she considered what to do she heard a sound which made her blood run cold. Footsteps, and they were coming up the stairs. Someone was coming up to the top landing. For a moment she froze and despite the heat, a cold sweat broke out on her brow;

Andrew. Surely he was not back from London yet! It was not time to wait and find out. Jumping to her feet Tara pulled the cupboard door closed, switched off the light and afraid whoever it was might investigate the cupboard, buried herself among Mrs Ward's dresses hanging on the rail at the end. She knew she was not well hidden, but hoped she might escape a cursory glance. Thank goodness all the cases and boxes were as she had found them; the only tell-tale was the heavy perfume in the air, but perhaps whoever it was would not be very perceptive or else imagine it came from Mrs Ward's clothes.

She could hear someone moving in the bedroom, the sound of the door closing, of the curtains being thrown back. Tara pressed herself against the wall behind the clothes rail and was suddenly aware of something digging into her back. Easing her hand round behind she located whatever it was in the darkness and explored it with her fingers. It was a door handle. There was another door out of the cupboard. She turned carefully and tried the handle. The door swung open to reveal more darkness. She could see absolutely nothing. Still afraid that Andrew, for she was certain it was he, might open the cupboard, Tara decided she might be safer on the other side of the unexpected door, whatever it concealed. Moving slowly to avoid unnecessary noise she eased her way round the door and closed it behind her. It was only a makeshift plywood door without a lock and she had no way of preventing it from being opened; all she could do was pray that if Andrew did investigate the cupboard the hidden door would remain hidden, for Tara had no illusions, she knew she was trapped.

She could hear nothing now of the movement in the bedroom, but was painfully aware any sound she made might be heard outside. She lowered herself on to the floor and with her back against the wall, waited.

As she sat in the dark hardly daring to breathe, there was an unexpected sound from inside the room, right beside her. It so startled her that she caught her breath with an audible gasp, and then clamped her hand over her mouth as she strained to hear if Andrew had been alerted. The noise which had alarmed her came again, a metallic sound, this time followed by a friendly gurgling. Tara found tears of relief starting in her eyes as she recognised the sound. It was a water tank. She must be in a tiny tank room blocked off from the end of the attic cupboard.

Anxious to allay her fears and prove it was only a tank, Tara stretched out her hand and discovered the tank not two feet from her. Realising she had not heard the tank from the outer part of the cupboard, Tara felt almost certain her gasp of fear would not have been heard on the other side of the door either, and she relaxed a little. But her relaxation was short-lived and every nerve in her body drew bowstring-tight as she heard someone in the dormer cupboard. There were bumps and thuds and then a loud snap, followed by scuffling and scraping. Tara retreated to the far corner of the tank room, squeezing herself in between the tank and the slope of the ceiling, and sitting on a large metal box which was wedged there already.

She was concentrating all her attention on the sounds coming from the other side of the door and it took some while for the significance of what she was sitting on to penetrate her mind, but as Tara tried to visualise movements which might explain the series of noises from outside in the cupboard, her fingers explored the edges of her perch, and encountered a small padlock. She was sitting on a padlocked metal box. A padlocked metal box. The sort of thing for which she had been searching. A flicker of hope stirred inside her and slipping off the box she ran her hands all over it. It was not large, about the size of a big cash box, with handles at each end, closed with a tongue and ring fastener and secured with a padlock. The more she considered her find the more Tara felt certain it was Jane's box. It was clear Mrs Ward had thrown away nothing that had belonged to Jane and yet fearing perhaps what the contents of the tin box might reveal about her daughter, she had hidden it away, denying its existence when the police made their original search for evidence.

Tara determined to carry the box down to her bedroom where she could study the contents at leisure. Her heart skipped a beat at the thought that she might be the one to discover the evidence to clear Simon's name.

But reality struck hard and her attention was drawn sharply back to her actual position. Through the door she heard voices. One she was sure was Paul's, the other, lower, was almost certainly Andrew's. She could not hear what was said, but after a moment there was silence. The tank muttered beside her but there was no sound from

195

outside in the cupboard. Tara pressed her ear to the door. Dare she open it? She was almost sure Andrew had gone for a moment. If so now was her chance to escape from the trap. Very slowly and gently she eased the door open and peeped out between the hanging clothes that partially concealed her. The light was still on in the cupboard but it was empty. Tara listened intently, but there was no sound from the room beyond. A quick glance told her that Andrew had been searching, too. The truck which had been locked now stood open, its metal clasps bent where force had been used, and a heap of furs lay tumbled on the floor. Ignoring the confusion, Tara slipped back into the tank room, retrieved the cash box from beside the tank and emerged once more into the bedroom. As she moved stealthily towards the door she heard footsteps on the stairs. Andrew was coming back. Fear paralysed Tara for a split second; she stood clutching her prize in the middle of the bedroom, poised for flight with nowhere to run; she would never regain the safety of the tank room quickly and quietly enough to escape detection, and Andrew could not fail to see her leaving the room from the top of the stairs if she made a dash for it. As the footsteps crossed the landing and approached the room, Tara darted behind the half-open door, the precious box still held firmly in her arms. What she would say in explanation when Andrew discovered her there she had no idea, but an instinct for self-preservation insisted that at least she try to hide.

Andrew strode into the room and without turning went straight across to the cupboard. With her heart pounding so loudly that she was sure he must hear it, Tara peeped round the edge of the door. Andrew was inside the dormer cupboard. Tara needed no second chances, in a flash she was out of the room and tiptoeing down the stairs to her own bedroom. Afraid that Andrew might have heard her flight and be at this minute immediately behind her, Tara rammed the box under her bed and collapsed on to the mattress, her whole body shaking, the blood drumming in her ears and her heart pounding like a steam-hammer.

There was no knock on her door and as the minutes passed undisturbed, Tara's reaction gradually subsided and she lay exhausted on her bed. She glanced at her watch and dragged herself to her feet. Mandy would be back anytime, and Tara wanted to be downstairs with every appearance of normality, for as she lay considering the events of the afternoon an added fear had come to her. Andrew had been searching for something, too; why else should he go through Jane's effects? So Andrew knew there was something worth finding, and Tara felt with sudden certainty that Andrew had been looking for Jane's records, too. But why he had only just started to search baffled her.

13

Fear sharpened her wits and Tara decided to make sure Andrew thought she had been out for the afternoon. She could no longer pretend she had been asleep in her room all afternoon, he could well have checked her bedroom earlier, the door had not been locked, indeed it was probable that he had.

Very softly she eased her door open. The landing was empty. She could hear the television on in the lounge and guessed Paul was watching the children's programmes. That was all to the good. With a final glance to be certain that the vital box was completely concealed under her bed, Tara crept out of her room, this time turning the key and slipping it into her pocket; then she sped downstairs through the deserted hall and out of the front door. She dared not use the garden entrance in case Andrew should see her from his window.

She walked briskly until she was out of sight of the house and then slowed her pace a little to stroll round the block and approach Old Court through the alley and the back gate. As she turned on to the promenade she had a curious feeling that she was being watched and looking over her shoulder she studied the crowds milling aimlessly about her as they enjoyed the afternoon sun, but no one seemed to be taking any interest in her. Perhaps it was Simon; Tara felt she would know if he were near. She paused by one of the fountains, perching on the low wall which surrounded it in case he was close by and wanted to speak to her. She watched the cool water splashing down into the tiled bowl beneath the fountain, the perpetual pattering calming her, the spray cooling her burning cheeks. There was no sign of Simon. Tara drew herself reluctantly away from the fountain and was about to turn her steps towards the guest house once more when she heard someone calling her name. It was Mandy, wearing her bikini and carrying a beach bag; having broiled herself a delicate lobster on the beach that afternoon she was returning to Old Court to help Tara with dinner. Mandy waved and Tara waited for her to catch up.

'So you did come out after all,' Mandy cried. 'Have you been looking for me?'

'No, not really,' replied Tara. 'I couldn't sleep so I decided to come out for some air. I've been window shopping in the High Street.'

Chatting together they threaded their way leisurely through the holidaymakers and branched off into the alley leading to the garden of Old Court. As they entered the gate Tara glanced up at the windows of the guest house which gave on to the courtyard. Andrew Harper was staring down into the paved garden, his eyes unseeing, lost in thought. Tara's heart beat faster, but anxious to establish the fact that she had been out for the afternoon she waved cheerily to him and Mandy, following her glance, waved as well. The movement drew his attention and he gave a perfuntory lift of his hand before he withdrew to the shadows of his room.

Tara and Mandy set about cooking dinner for the guests, and while Mandy laid out the cold starters they had prepared earlier, Tara went up to the television lounge to find out what Paul wanted for his tea.

'Did you have a good day, Paul?' she asked. 'How was London?'

'Didn't see much,' answered the boy without glancing away from the television screen. 'Went to see Gran on the way home, at least Uncle Andrew did. I wasn't allowed in.'

'Did he say how she was?' enquired Tara gently. 'Was she better?'

'Don't know. I didn't see her.' At last Paul turned away from the whirling cartoon he had been watching and added, 'She liked my card. He said she liked it. It was by her bed.'

'I'm sure she loved it,' said Tara. 'You spent a long time on making it. Do you want some supper now? Have you eaten anything?'

'Uncle Andrew did say we could have tea in a cafe, but when he'd seen Gran he said there wasn't time after all and we had to come home. I've had a biscuit, that's all.'

'Beans on toast?'

'Yes, please,' said Paul enthusiastically. 'Can I have an egg on top?' Tara laughed. 'I should think we could run to that. I'll give you a call.'

As she went back down to the kitchen she was accosted by an irate Andrew.

'Tara! Someone's been in my room today. I left it locked and came back to find it not only unlocked but with the door open.'

Tara had realised that this point would have to be explained and had her explanation ready. She turned to him calmly.

'Yes, I went in. I went in to do the bed and clean, I thought you'd prefer I did it rather than Mrs Vernon. Anyway when I found it was locked I used the spare key. I saw you'd made the bed so I concluded that you didn't want the usual guest house services, so I left the room as it was.'

'Why didn't you lock the door again?' demanded Andrew.

'Didn't I?' Tara spoke with innocent surprise. 'I thought I had. I must have forgotten. I'm sorry. Did it matter?' Though she spoke coolly, Tara's heart thudded painfully. 'Anyway we won't go into your room again. I'll tell Mandy.' She turned away casually and continued down to the kitchen, leaving Andrew staring angrily after her.

Tara's mind was far from the dining room that evening as she served the guests' dinner. While fetching vegetables and clearing plates she went over and over the events of the day, trying to set them in order, to establish some sort of pattern from the snippets she had. Apart from her own discovery of a metal box which might or might not contain the evidence Simon needed, her main preoccupation was with Andrew and his movements. He had gone to London as planned but had not stayed long. Then on the way home he had stopped at the hospital to visit Mrs Ward. She was still too ill for Paul to be allowed in to see her, yet Andrew had changed his plans after his visit; instead of taking Paul out for the promised tea, he had rushed back to Old Court and started searching through the things in the dormer cupboard. The more she considered this the more Tara became convinced that despite her condition, Andrew had told the old lady that Paul's father had reappeared. But what could she have said to occasion such frantic activity on Andrew's part? Surely it could only be that she had confided in Andrew at last and actually admitted to having papers of Jane's which Simon might try to find. However, if that were the case why did he not discover the box and Tara tucked away in the tank room?

A wave of horror flooded through her as a reason presented itself. Perhaps the box she had found had nothing to do with Jane. Perhaps she had missed something when searching the boxes and cases in the outer cupboard. Until now Tara had planned to greet Simon later, triumphantly carrying the tin cash box, so that they could open it together. This idea, reviewed in cold reality, was an obvious non-starter; first on a practical level because it would be almost impossible to leave Old Court unobserved and a large black metal box must occasion some comment, particularly if Andrew recognised it as what he was looking for, and second she now wanted to investigate the contents of the box before raising any hopes in Simon.

Having made this decision Tara was itching to get back upstairs to tackle the padlock. To be certain no one else attempted this before her, she removed the spare key to her own room from the hook in the kitchen and slipped it into the box of purple and pink petunias on the outside sill.

'Tara! You're miles away!' Mandy's amused voice penetrated her thoughts at last. 'You haven't heard a word I've said, have you?'

'Sorry,' smiled Tara. 'You're right, I was miles away. What did you say?'

'Nothing of tremendous importance,' grinned Mandy. 'I just said I was going out now, to see that man I met on the beach.'

'What man?'

'I told you. He was on the blanket next to mine and I've agreed to meet him for a drink this evening.'

'Oh, I see,' said Tara who had no recollection whatsoever of the earlier conversation. 'Well, have a nice time. Watch it though, being picked up by beachcombers.'

Mandy laughed. 'Don't worry, I will,' and disappeared upstairs to change. Tara finished laying the breakfast tables and then followed.

Once having gained the security of her own room she turned the key and safe from unexpected interruption, dragged the tin from under her bed. Now faced with it Tara found she was quite unable to open it. The tongue was a thick strip of metal riveted in place, and the ring over which it passed was steel. The padlock was not large, but sturdy. Without the key or someone with a jemmy and more strength than Tara, there was no way into the box from that approach. She turned her attention to the hinges, but the lid was hinged from the inside and there was no chance of breaking in from there.

In frustration Tara picked up the box and shook it. The contents did not rattle and the whole thing was not particularly heavy, most of the weight belonging to the box rather than what it contained. Papers. It must hold papers and it was papers for which Tara was hunting. More determined than ever she set the box down on her bedroom chair and walked round it in the vain hope of inspiration. She glanced out of the window and saw the dusk creeping over the surrounding roof tops, chimneys standing stark against the fading orange of the sky, windows yellow squares of artificial light. She crossed to her own open window, about to draw the curtains and saw the figure of Mandy crossing the courtyard to the garden gate.

As she disappeared into the alley beyond Tara longed to follow her. Simon would be waiting at the other end, leaning on the sea wall as he had two nights ago. Was it only two nights since she had, with tremendous apprehension, slipped out to meet him? A surge of longing for him overwhelmed her. Damn Jane's box, she would go now, meet him anyway. Jane's box. Jane's box! The words echoed in her head and an elusive memory danced at the back of her mind, pulled her up short. Jane's box. Why did those particular two words set her searching the recesses of her mind, and why was it essential that she should pin down their sudden significance? She must have said them a hundred times before without producing the echo.

Calmly and deliberately Tara made herself sit down on the bed, and relaxing, allowed her brain to slide over the story of Jane Hamilton, but to no avail. Sighing, she decided to let the memory slip into focus in its own time, and reaching for her keys she stood up to unlock her door. It was the sight of the tab on the room key that tripped the switch in her mind; in that instant Tara remembered where she had heard the words 'Jane's box'; not heard indeed, but seen. On a loose key tab in Mrs Ward's bag, she had seen it when looking for Andrew's phone number. It was so simple Tara could hardly believe she had not thought of it at once. The key to the padlock was in Mrs Ward's handbag, which was itself in Mrs Ward's bedroom. Andrew Harper's bedroom, now. Her heart sank as quickly as it had risen and Tara nearly wept with frustration. If only she had thought, if only she had realised while she was actually in Andrew's room that afternoon.

Still, that couldn't be helped; now she must devise a way of getting hold of Mrs Ward's bunch of keys. But where was Andrew? Tara had replaced the spare key to his room on the board in the kitchen, she had only to fetch it and wait for Andrew to leave his room and it would be the work of a minute to remove the keys from the handbag.

Swiftly Tara went down to the kitchen. She could hear the television on. Perhaps luck would really be with her and Andrew would be in the lounge watching with Paul. She crossed to the key board and raised her hand to take Andrew's key, then she froze. It was not there. Quickly she scanned the other hooks to see if she had misplaced it when returning it earlier, but she had not. The spare key to Andrew's room had gone. Perhaps annoyed at her admitted invasion of his room earlier and fearing further intrusion, he had taken the extra key, as Tara had hidden the extra key to her own room.

Tara's spirits plummeted, as she stood staring at the empty hook. The door opened behind her and she spun round to find Paul standing there dressed in his pyjamas.

'I'm going to bed now,' he said. 'Will you come and read me a story?'

Tara smiled at him; still so pale-faced he seemed to have shrunk somehow in the last few days.

'Of course,' she said, sounding more cheerful than she felt. 'You go and get into bed and I'll be up in a minute.' Then the germ of an idea crept into her mind and she said casually, 'Where's Uncle Andrew?'

The child shrugged. 'Don't know. In his bedroom I think.'

'I see,' said Tara. 'Well, you go on up and choose a story and I'll be right there.' She glanced into the television lounge on the way upstairs. A family was ranged before the set laughing at a comedy show, but there was no sign of Andrew.

Tara read Paul his story and then tucked him in.

'Will I be able to go and see Gran soon?' he asked as she bent to kiss him goodnight.

'I don't know, Paul. You'll have to ask Uncle Andrew. I'll get him to come in and say goodnight to you now and you can see what he says. See you in the morning.' Leaving Paul's light on she stepped out on to the landing, and before calling Andrew, opened the linen cupboard. She needed an excuse to remain on the upstairs landing for a minute or two. She took a deep breath and trying to stop her hands from shaking, Tara knocked on Andrew's door. After a moment which was long enough to make Tara raise her hand to knock again, Andrew opened the door and glowered at her.

'Yes?'

'Paul wants you to go in and say goodnight to him.'

'Is he in bed?'

'Yes, I've read his story, he just wants to say goodnight, and,' she added, to be sure the subject arose and Andrew was detained long enough, 'he needs reassuring about his grandmother.'

Andrew grunted and went into Paul's room. In a flash Tara was into Andrew's bedroom and over to the bedside table where Mrs Ward's handbag had been. For an instant her heart stopped as she realised it was not there, but looking wildly around her, she saw it on top of a pile of Mrs Ward's possessions which Andrew had unceremoniously heaped in a corner. She darted over to it and unwilling to take the bag itself in case Andrew noticed its disappearance, spent precious seconds opening it and hunting for the keys. Her fingers encountered the ring and with a sigh of relief she stuffed the heavy bunch of keys into her pocket and made for the door. She reached the linen cupboard and began removing towels at random so that when Andrew paused at Paul's

214

door to switch off the light, Tara was carrying an unwanted pile of freshly laundered towels down to the landing below, with the vital keys at last in her possession.

14

Once safely back in her own bedroom, Tara locked the door and with mounting excitement turned to the intriguing metal box. She produced the bunch of keys and found as she tried each key in turn that her hands were shaking.

The fourth key fitted, turned easily and with a click the padlock sprang open. Tara took it off and levered the tongue of the clasp clear of the metal ring. She raised the lid and looked inside.

The box was made like a small filing cabinet with cardboard dividers lettered through the alphabet. Between each of these, various papers and large brown envelopes were filed. Tara drew out the only paper and envelope filed under A. Both had the name John Adams on them neatly written in block capitals. The paper appeared to be a balance sheet of some sort, with dates down one side and amounts of money set against them. Tara, puzzled, set it aside and opened the envelope. Inside were a smaller envelope and several photographs of a middle-aged man performing some most athletic feats on a bed with a beautiful girl, Jane, clad only in a policeman's helmet. The small envelope contained the negatives and a piece of paper with the man's address, and personal details on it together with the names of his family, of the company he worked for and explicit comments as to the exact nature of Mr John Adam's sexual pro-clivities.

Tara stared at the papers and photographs spread out before her, and realised with a sickening horror that Jane Hamilton had been more than a whore, she had been a very successful blackmailer. With sudden revulsion Tara stuffed the sordid evidence back into its envelope and slipped it back into the file.

'Well,' she breathed, 'this certainly

provides a motive for someone wanting to get rid of that bitch.'

She glanced back into the file. There were a fair number of envelopes. Were they all victims of Jane's, paying out blackmail money to protect themselves from her and their own weaknesses? Tara flipped through the file, looking at the names on the envelopes. One or two were familiar, prominent people who must have become entrapped by the beautiful Jane Hamilton. Tara did not open any more of the envelopes until she came to one which brought her heart to a standstill. It was labelled Andrew Harper. With trembling fingers she opened the large envelope and discovered as before a smaller envelope and some photographs, glossy enlargements. Andrew's pleasure appeared to be small boys. The child in the picture was not more than eleven or twelve. Jane did not feature in these photographs, but the bedroom in which they were taken was clearly the same room as in the first picture. Tara added another to Jane's list of vices, that of procuring children for her customers. The small envelope contained the negatives as before and various addresses including the Law Society. Andrew was not married, but his mother's name was listed and those of the partners in his firm. The balance sheet revealed that over a period of two years, Andrew had paid Jane something in the order of three and a half thousand pounds. So Andrew was a victim of Jane's, too. Tara felt a wave of fear pass through her and glanced round nervously at the closed door. Andrew was upstairs. He was searching for something and Tara had no doubt now as to what it was that he was looking for.

Galvanized into action by the sudden thought of Andrew discovering the tank room and probably some signs of her having been in it, Tara stuffed the photographs of Andrew back into the envelope. Quickly she thumbed through the file and selected the envelopes labelled with names of a judge and a cabinet minister; then she closed and locked the box and looked round the room for somewhere to hide it. There was nowhere, at least nowhere which was not so obvious as to reveal itself to the most inefficient searcher.

Should I take it with me, after all? wondered Tara, but discarded the idea. She had only to meet Andrew on the way out and everything would be lost. She must do the best she could. Her eye rested on her suitcase tucked tidily under the bed. It would have to do.

It was the work of a moment to lock the metal box into her case and return it under the bed; then Tara put on her anorak, despite the warmth of the evening and concealed the three vital envelopes inside it, tucking them tightly beneath her left arm so that at a casual glance she was carrying nothing. Quietly she opened her door, pausing a moment before emerging on to the landing, then softly she closed and locked it behind her. As she started for the head of the stairs she heard a door bang and footsteps on the landing above. Andrew was on his way down. Her fear turned to panic and careless of the noise she made Tara pelted down the stairs and dived out of the front door into the warm and dusty street. Having lost control of her fear for a moment Tara kept running, her feet resounding on the pavement, her breath coming in painful gasps.

She reached the neon lights of the High Street and slowed a little as she encountered the mildly interested glances of strolling holidaymakers, and as she did so she thought she caught the sound of footsteps running behind her. She spun round, terrified, expecting to see Andrew looming out of the gloom, but it was only a young woman running across the road to avoid an oncoming car. With aching relief, Tara turned for the promenade and forcing herself to think calmly once again she walked purposefully to where Simon would be waiting.

He sat on the sea wall, his eyes fixed on the alley way which led to the back entrance of Old Court, as if afraid he might miss Tara in the deepening dusk. For a moment she paused to look at him, Simon Hamilton, the man she intended to marry and her heart contracted with love as she noticed again the deep lines that worry had etched on his face.

The moment passed and Tara stepped closer to him, close enough for him to be aware of her and he swung round. The lines from his face vanished in sudden pleasure as he saw her. For an instant he clasped her in his arms and then said crisply, 'Well?'

'We must go somewhere where we can sit and talk,' said Tara urgently. 'So much has happened.'

'The dunes?'

'No,' Tara shook her head, 'I've got things to show you, we need light; a quiet corner in a pub would do.'

Simon nodded and took her arm. Together they joined the drifting holidaymakers who strolled arm in arm along the promenade admiring the illuminations or watching the moon rise out of the sea. But finding a quiet corner in a pub in Silverstrand during high season was no easy task, and it was some time before they found a likely place, a bar near the station, called The Railway Inn.

Twice as they had turned a corner Tara thought she heard footsteps behind her, but she saw no one when she looked back uneasily.

'What's the matter?' asked Simon sharply.

'Nothing really,' said Tara cautiously, 'I just have this feeling we're being followed.'

'Who by?'

Tara shrugged. 'I don't know, some-one working for Andrew perhaps?'

'Andrew? Tara what the hell is going on?'

'I'll tell you inside.'

The lounge bar of the Railway Inn was almost empty. Tara took over a small table in a corner where they could sit with a clear view of the door. Simon bought them each a brandy and joined her.

'Now then,' he said. 'What's this all about? What has been happening in the last couple of days?'

Silently Tara produced the envelopes she had concealed under her anorak and placed them on the table in front of him. Simon stared at them for a moment and then with shaking hands picked up the top one labelled with the name of Andrew Harper. As he withdrew the papers and photographs from inside Tara whispered urgently, 'Be careful. Don't let anyone see.' And while Simon perused the contents of that envelope and the other two, Tara kept her eyes firmly on the door, for she still had the uneasy feeling that they had been followed.

A low whistle escaped Simon. 'Christ, Tara!' he rasped. 'This is dynamite. Where did you get all this?'

'I've found Jane's box. There are lots more envelopes; she must have been blackmailing all of them.' Tara shuddered. 'You were right, Simon, she was evil; evil through to her soul.'

'I doubt if she had one,' said Simon mildly. 'You know, she must have had a concealed camera somewhere in that bedroom of hers, or perhaps an accomplice who watched through that mirror and took pictures which looked promising for blackmail; though she was unlikely to want to share the proceeds. More likely there was an automatic device she could work herself.'

Tara shuddered again at the thought of so perverted an act and Simon quickly returned the photographs to their respective envelopes and then he said, 'Now drink your brandy and tell me everything.' So Tara took a pull at her drink and fortified a little by the fire it brought inside her, related to Simon the events of the last two days. He listened without interrupting, his glass clasped in his hands, his drink untasted and forgotten; but his expression reflected his anxiety when he heard how Paul had tried to run away.

'Poor little kid,' he muttered. 'Nothing breaks his way.'

Tara continued her story and when she had described how Andrew had come back unexpectedly during the afternoon she added, 'Paul said he'd been in to see Mrs Ward. She must have told him about Jane's box, and now he's looking for it.'

Simon nodded. 'If he'd known before he'd have looked before.'

'But he must have known,' pointed out Tara. 'I mean, he knew he was being blackmailed, so he must have known the pictures were somewhere.'

'But not that Mrs Ward had them. Remember she denied all knowledge of them and there was no real reason to disbelieve her; would you leave that sort of stuff with your mother? Only Jane would do something like that. Now Mrs Ward's terrified because I'm back on the scene and may be able to take Paul from her and expose Jane for what she really was, so not knowing of Andrew's personal involvement, she's asked him to find the box.'

'But why didn't he come straight to it, in that case?' asked Tara with a shiver. 'He'd have found me, too.'

'She's very ill, don't forget. Perhaps she just said in the cupboard, or in a cupboard. You didn't find the tank room immediately did you?'

'No. I suppose that could explain it. She wasn't very articulate when I went to see her, I must say. But what'll he do when he can't find the box?'

'What would you do?'

'Search the rest of the house in case, and then go back to Mrs Ward; ask her to be more explicit.' Tara sighed. 'But any one of those people could have murdered Jane, or arranged for her death. I don't suppose any of them is short of cash, and lots must have been in a position where a breath of scandal could destroy them.'

'That doesn't matter, don't you see?' cried Simon. 'These,' he tapped the envelopes, 'these may be enough to have the enquiry re-opened. They're entirely new evidence, suppressed evidence at that. If we can produce them in court it may even be enough to clear me.'

Tara felt suddenly as if an enormous weight had been lifted from her; the relief from the burden she had been carrying made her feel light-headed, almost tipsy. She turned to Simon with shining eyes, all the love she bore him illuminating her face and she whispered, 'Oh, Simon, do you really think so?'

For a moment he was overcome by the expression he caught on her face and grasping her hand he pressed it to his lips.

'I hope so, my darling. I hope and pray so.'

'So,' said Tara, suddenly brisk, 'what do we do now?'

'I'm not sure,' admitted Simon. 'I mean, I don't know how to go about getting the enquiry re-opened. I think the best thing is for me to take these envelopes to my solicitor. He'll know what to do. Incidentally, he actually believed my story, too.'

'What about the box?' asked Tara. 'That's not in the least safe where it is.'

'There's nowhere else you can put it, is there?'

'Not in the house.'

'Look, I'll go up to London tomorrow and see my solicitor, Peter Alton. He'll know what to do. If I catch the earliest train possible, I can be back during the afternoon and I'll phone and tell you what he says we're to do next, about the box and things.'

'I won't leave Old Court tomorrow until you've rung. It'll be more difficult for Andrew to search if I'm about all day.'

'And try and keep Paul with you,' said Simon darkly. 'I don't want him left with Andrew if we can possibly avoid it.'

Tara thought of the photographs and shuddered. 'No. Don't worry, I'll do my best to keep him with me.'

Simon went to the bar to refill their

glasses and Tara relaxed back into her chair, thankful that she had passed on responsibility for the evidence to Simon. True there was more hidden in her room at Old Court, but even if Andrew did discover and destroy that, Tara felt sure that the envelopes Simon now had would be enough to re-open enquiries and perhaps lead to the clearing of Simon's name.

The door from the public bar swung open and a woman came through. She crossed to a chair by the window and seating herself, opened her bag, found and lit a cigarette and settled back comfortably, smoking. Tara watched her with quickening interest. She had seen her before; something about her was familiar. Tara sought for recognition but the memory eluded her. As if aware of Tara's scrutiny the woman looked up and for a moment returned the stare, but there was no recognition in her look and colouring a little, Tara turned away. When Simon returned with the drinks she said softly, 'Don't turn round now, but when you can, take a look at that woman in the corner. I know her from somewhere, but I can't think where.'

Simon eased himself round casually and took a quick glance at the woman who was looking at her watch, waiting for someone. He shrugged.

'I've never seen her before,' he said. He turned back to Tara and took her hand. 'Now listen,' he said, 'I've been thinking. Take the rest of the records out of the tin box and put them into something else, then if Andrew does find the box he still won't have the evidence. Leave the box locked and with luck even if he does get hold of it by the time he's forced it open we'll have these envelopes lodged with my solicitor.'

'Why don't you take my car?' suggested Tara suddenly. 'You could drive up to London tonight, and see your man first thing in the morning.'

Simon considered for a moment and then shook his head. 'No,' he said, 'Andrew might notice the car missing and if he hasn't tied you in with what's going on, we don't want to alert him.'

With the vital documents safely tucked inside Simon's jacket, they left the pub and arm in arm strolled back towards the guest house, like any other holidaymakers. As they reached the corner of Grove Road, Tara suddenly clutched Simon's arm more tightly and stopped dead.

'Simon! That woman! The one in the pub.'

'What about her?'

'I've remembered where I saw her. It was here, on this corner. I was running and when I looked back she was running, too.'

'Running after you?'

'I don't know. I thought so for a moment, but she ran across the road and went the other way.'

'But she could have turned back and followed you?'

Tara nodded miserably.

'Was she in the bar when you gave me the envelopes?'

Tara shook her head. 'No, she came in when you went up to get the second lot of drinks.'

'Then if she was following, all she knows is that we met. She won't have seen the envelopes because I'd already put them away.' Simon put his hands on Tara's shoulders and looked down into her white and frightened face.

'Don't worry, darling. It may have been coincidence; in fact it probably was, you're just a bit nervy, that's all.' Simon tried to sound reassuring but they both knew in their hearts that such a coincidence was most improbable.

As before, in the sheltering shadow of the plane tree they said goodnight and with Simon's parting words, 'I love you Tara. I love you and need you,' still sounding in her ears, Tara turned with a light step towards Old Court.

15

Tara let herself into the quiet house and slipped upstairs to her room, hoping she would encounter no one on the way. The dim landing light burned as usual and she could see several bedroom doors still had lines of light beneath them, but she met nobody and relieved, she slid her key into the lock of her bedroom door. As she reached for the light switch Tara suddenly knew that something was wrong; flicking on the light she gasped in horror. Her room was in utter confusion. Terrified she spun round, afraid someone was behind her, but the landing was empty and the house was still. In a sudden rush of panic, Tara closed the door and fumbling the key into the keyhole, turned the lock. She leaned against the door for a moment, her heart pounding, her eyes closed against the chaos of her room and the knowledge that the precious tin box would no longer be there.

Tara drew a deep breath and forced herself to open her eyes and face the truth. Andrew had found the box, the battered suitcase with clasps wrenched free testified to that. Jane's box had gone and Andrew had not bothered to conceal his search. Drawers were upended, their contents strewn upon the floor; the wardrobe door hung open and Tara's few dresses were heaped on the carpet. The bedclothes had been ripped off the bed and tossed over the single chair and the suitcase which had contained the box lay upside down by the window. It looked like the work of a madman. The hope that Andrew had not connected Tara with the missing box was exploded and she was left with the frightening knowledge that once he had managed to force open the box, he would be back to discover from her the whereabouts of the missing envelope.

Tara considered calling the police,

treating the affair as a break-in, but she discarded the idea almost at once. There was no evidence to tie Andrew in with it and she might never have the chance to regain the box, if fear of the police pushed Andrew into getting rid of it. Also she realised she would have to admit searching Mrs Ward's cupboards and removing a box which did not belong to her, and that would almost certainly complicate matters. At least Andrew could claim he was searching on behalf of Mrs Ward. She knew, too, that Simon did not want the police brought in until he had been to see his solicitor and knew what help the new evidence might be.

Mechanically Tara began to clear up the mess, and as she hung her dresses back into the wardrobe and folded her clothes back into the drawers, her mind in tumult churned over and over what she should do. What could she do? Andrew had the box and once he discovered his own file missing from it he would be back.

Tara longed to run; to get right away from Old Court, it was obviously the safest move, but if she did how would Simon find her? Could she find him? She knew now he was staying with a Mrs Willard in Jubilee Crescent, but she had no idea what number Jubilee Crescent. She knew there was no phone and so short of knocking on all the doors in the road and asking there was no way she could find out. She could hardly do that at midnight and by morning Simon would be gone. She sighed and tears sprang to her eyes, she felt very alone and very vulnerable. She did not even know with any certainty where Jubilee Crescent was and her fear of Andrew made her most unwilling to venture out by herself into the night to look for it.

On the whole, perhaps she was safer in the guest house where there were people at hand. Surely Andrew would not be able to harm her there; and she only had to wait until Simon phoned tomorrow afternoon. If she was left alone in the house for any reason during the coming day, she would lock herself into her room for safety. But that safety was illusory, and she stiffened again as she realised it. Andrew must have a key to her room. How else had he got in to search it? She had left it locked and it was still locked when she returned. The cold truth had to be faced, she had no refuge.

She looked round her wildly for a moment and then darted across to the chair. Tipping the bedclothes off it she carried it to the door and wedged its back under the handle. Now at least Andrew Harper could not slip in unheralded. Fortified a little by this thought, Tara went to bed, but though she tried to sleep she only managed to doze fitfully, waking with a start every time she heard a sound, and when she got up next morning and peered into her mirror, it was a grey, drawn face which stared back at her.

Mandy was already in the kitchen

frying bacon when Tara went down-stairs. She glanced up and smiled as Tara came in.

'Morning,' she called cheerfully. 'Sleep well?' She registered Tara's pale face and added, 'No, I can see you didn't. You look awful!'

Tara managed a weak grin. 'Thanks for the vote of confidence, really morale boosting!'

Mandy laughed. 'Sorry,' she said, 'but you do look a bit peaky.'

'I feel it,' admitted Tara. 'I think I'll probably go back to bed for a couple of hours later on. See if I can sleep off this headache.'

'Good idea,' agreed Mandy. 'Go back now if you like. I can cope here. Oh, by the way, Mr Harper went to London last night. He left sometime after you went out. He was leaving as I came back. Disaster, my date was. You were right about beachcombers! One drink with that guy was quite enough. What a bore! Fishing was his thing, on and on, and here's me trying to look intelligent and think of a way to escape.'

'Did he say anything?' asked Tara, paying no attention to Mandy's account of her evening.

'Who? The beachcomber?'

'No,' snapped Tara, 'Andrew Harper.'

Mandy raised a quizzical eyebrow at her tone and answered calmly, 'He said he'd be back in a day or two, something about getting power of attorney for Mrs Ward. Once she's signed he can act for her in everything legal. We won't be needed. He's going to close the guest house completely until Mrs Ward is well enough to run it again.'

Tara stared at Mandy. 'Can he do that? What about Paul?'

'He said something about Paul going to a prep school, as a boarder.' Mandy shrugged her shoulders, 'I don't really know about that, all I do know is that he won't need either of us after Saturday.'

Tara was stunned by the news, turning it over in her mind as she helped Mandy cook and serve the breakfast. She had very mixed feelings about it all and longed to question Mandy further, but did not want to draw undue attention to her interest. Andrew must feel completely secure now he had the box. At least he was out of the house and in the immediate future she was safe, but it also meant that Simon had very little time to establish himself as a fit person to look after Paul. If he got held up or was unable to see his solicitor that day, Andrew might return with the power of attorney in his pocket and carry the boy off with him, leading to a legal wrangle to get Paul back. Paul! The thought struck her. Where was Paul now? He had not appeared for breakfast.

'Where's Paul now?' Tara demanded of Mandy as they passed in the hall carrying trays of breakfast to and from the dining room.

'He went with Mr Harper,' replied Mandy.

'Andrew got him out of bed to go with him?'

'Poor kid, he did look a bit bleary, but Mr Harper was worried about Paul's father turning up. The child's terrified of him you know; the father I mean.'

Tara's heart sank. Andrew already had Paul; then a flicker of hope revived. After all, the photographs would prove without doubt that Andrew was no fit person to have charge of the boy. Perhaps, after all, it would not be so difficult to get Paul back.

The rest of the morning passed peacefully, though painfully slowly for Tara. At last lunch was served and cleared away and Mandy, looking out at another brilliant day, announced she was going to the beach.

'After all, if we're only here until Saturday we might as well make the most of it. Coming to protect me from my beachcomber?'

Tara shook her head, thinking wryly that it was she who was probably more likely to need protection. 'No, thanks, I think I'll try and catch up on some sleep; you were right, I didn't sleep well last night.' If she had realised how true her thoughts might turn out, Tara would never have let Mandy leave the house.

Once alone she did indeed go upstairs, but before she went into her own room she went up to Mrs Ward's bedroom, where Andrew had been. As she had half expected, the door was locked and the key still missing. Tara went back down to her room and, leaving the door ajar so that she would hear the telephone when Simon rang, she flung herself on to her bed and for the first time for several days relaxed completely. She was asleep in an instant.

She awoke sometime later with a start and uttered a cry of fear as she saw she was not alone. Her bedroom door was closed and leaning against it, with a small automatic pistol in his hand, was Andrew Harper. For a moment Tara was mesmerised by the black barrel of the gun pointing straight at her, paralysed like a rabbit facing a snake; and Andrew, with the cold emotionless eyes of such a snake stood and regarded her.

'So,' he said at last, 'I think you have something of mine.'

'What? I don't know what you mean.' Tara took refuge in feigned ignorance.

'Don't play dumb with me, my girl,' snarled Andrew. 'You know bloody well what I'm talking about. Where's that envelope?' He took a step towards her and Tara cowered back on the bed.

'Answer me!' he shrieked and his hand flashed out and dealt her a stinging blow across the side of her head.

Tara cried out, terrified, looking wildly for escape, but her glance at the door was intercepted by Andrew and he snapped, 'It's locked and the house is empty. Now where is it?' He hit her again so violently that her head jerked back and her vision clouded.

'I don't know,' she cried, flinging up her arms to protect herself from the third blow. 'I don't know. I haven't got it. I swear I haven't got it.'

'Then who has? Don't pretend with me. You took it from that box and you passed it on. Who's got it now?' The fourth blow caught her unprepared and set her ears singing and her head spinning.

'Simon!' she whispered with a spark of defiance. 'Simon Hamilton's got it.'

'Has he indeed? When I heard you'd met him again last night I rather thought there might be more to it than a lovers' tryst.' Andrew spoke the last words with a derisory laugh and Tara shuddered at the sound.

'What makes you think I met him last night? I just went out for a walk,' she retorted, still bravely defiant.

Andrew laughed again. 'Think? I don't think, I know for sure. I had you followed. You've had a shadow ever since I knew you were involved with Hamilton.'

'And when was that?'

'The moment you heard who he was.

Your face read like an open book.'

Remembering the evening among the dunes Tara was horrified at the thought of silent spectators. 'And you've had me followed since then? You bastard!' she spat.

'Now, now,' admonished Andrew, the mildness of his tone was belied by the clenching of his fist, 'language from a lady! Or perhaps you're no lady. Consorting with Hamilton's type, it seems unlikely.'

Tara ignored the taunt; she recognised her danger and felt Andrew itching to hit her again.

'They didn't pick you up until after you'd been rutting among the sand dunes,' continued Andrew, choosing his words carefully to cause her the maximum offence in the hope of provoking her, 'but I wasn't interested in your sordid sex life so it didn't matter. However, since you returned to civilisation that night I've known your every move outside this place.

'Now we must consider things as

they stand. Hamilton has something I want and I . . . '

'He's taken it to his solicitor. You're too late.' A note of triumph crept into Tara's voice as she interrupted him.

'Am I indeed? We'll see about that. Perhaps we can do a deal.' Andrew laughed harshly.

'He won't deal with you, you — ' began Tara with spirit. Andrew struck her again and she felt blood trickling down the side of her face.

'He will,' said Andrew softly, 'because I have Paul. Your lover,' Andrew spoke with contempt, 'your lover is a weak man. He always was a weak man. Jane Hamilton danced all over him, she ground his stupid face into the dirt.'

Tara longed to say, 'She did the same to you, Andrew Harper,' but she knew he would only hit her again and bit back the words. Her face was already swollen and bruised and the gash above her ear was still oozing blood.

'And now I suppose we must wait to hear from him. He is going to contact you, isn't he?' Andrew stepped menacingly towards her and she nodded wearily.

'Get up!' he jerked the gun at her and Tara staggered to her feet, the movement causing her head to spin again, so that she had to clutch the bed-head to steady herself. Andrew pulled a silencer from his pocket and, without taking his eyes from her, screwed it on to the automatic.

'You are of little use to me,' he spoke grimly. 'If you do not do exactly as I say I shall shoot; not to kill at first, but I'm sure you don't want to be crippled for the rest of your life. Understand?'

Tara, speechless, nodded.

'Good. Now upstairs to the old lady's room. We'll wait for the call there.'

With the gun prodding in her back, Tara scrambled up the second flight of stairs to Mrs Ward's bedroom. Andrew unlocked the door and with a shove sent her sprawling inside. As she crawled to her hands and knees Tara became aware of Paul sitting on a chair, his eyes enormous in his pale face, with a gag round his mouth and his arms tied to the arms of the chair.

'Paul!' she cried out and started towards him.

'Leave him,' hissed Andrew, 'and get on the bed.' Tara, afraid for both herself and the child, did as she was told.

'Now, pull down your jeans.'

'No!' Tara's anger and revulsion overcame her fear. Andrew gave a short unpleasant laugh.

'You'll be quite safe, I'm not interested in your beautiful body. You revolt me as I revolt you. Just pull them down round your ankles.' And as Tara still hesitated he crossed over to Paul and raising his hand to strike the petrified boy, said persuasively, 'Paul would like you to, wouldn't you Paul?'

She knew that Andrew would not hesitate to beat the little boy, and so reluctantly Tara unzipped her jeans and pushed them down round her ankles. She felt extremely vulnerable with her legs and panties thus exposed, but she realised that it was merely a device to hinder her movements, to prevent any sudden dash for the door, and she closed her mind to the snake-eyed Andrew's unemotional gaze.

How long they sat there all three trapped in a macabre still-life, Tara had no idea. It seemed like hours, but at last the terrible silence that smothered them was ripped apart by the jangle of the telephone. The waiting was over.

'Now,' said Andrew softly, 'you give him no warning or the boy will suffer. Answer it. Don't tell him you've lost the box; remember, I'm listening.'

Trembling, Tara picked up the receiver and whispered, 'Hallo.'

'Tara? Is that you?'

'Yes,' her voice was husky and with one eye on Andrew caressing Paul's kneecap with the tip of the gun she cleared her throat and said more clearly, 'Yes, it's me.'

'Are you all right, darling?' Simon was anxious. 'You sound funny.'

'I'm fine, really.'

'Great. Everything's going to be all right, Tara. It's going to be all right. I've seen Peter Alton, he's come down with me.' He sounded as exuberant as a boy escaped from school, all his excitement and happiness overflowing into his voice so that Tara's heart contracted at the thought of what he was soon to learn. Simon went on, exultant, 'We're at the Grand. Can you bring the box?'

'Yes, yes, of course.'

'Come now. I'm in room 306.' He paused, puzzled or even hurt at Tara's lack of enthusiasm and said gently, 'I love you, Tara.'

'I love you, Simon.' She replaced the receiver.

Andrew sneered, 'How very touching. Sounds as if you're going to be stuck with Tara as a stepmother, Paul. Now, what did he say?' Any idea that Tara had of keeping Simon's whereabouts secret was shattered by Andrew's attentions to Paul and she answered sullenly, 'Grand Hotel, room

251

306, I'm to go at once and take the box.'

'How sensible,' purred Andrew, moving to the door. 'We'll go together. You can drive.' He slipped a raincoat over his arm to conceal the gun which was once again pointed at Tara's stomach and turned the key in the lock. 'I should pull your trousers up now,' he added, 'you don't want to be conspicuous, do you?'

Tara struggled with her jeans. 'What about Paul?' she asked.

'Paul? Oh, he can stay here. You're not going anywhere, Paul, are you?' Tears were streaming down the little boy's face and despite the gun Tara went over to him and put her arms round him.

'Don't cry, Paul. Be brave. Daddy and I will be back to find you as soon as we can, I promise. Daddy's a good, brave man. We'll come to help you as soon as we can.' Deliberately she reached round and untied the handkerchief that gagged him. 'He'll suffocate if he goes on crying,' she said defiantly.

'The gag stays off.'

Andrew shrugged. 'No one'll hear him up here,' he said and then losing his patience snapped, 'Now get out and remember Simon won't want to marry a cripple.' Then with a final glance at the sobbing Paul still tied to the chair, he closed the bedroom door and locked it behind him, cutting off the sound of the sobs and leaving the terrified child alone.

16

The journey across town to the Grand Hotel was not a pleasant one. Tara drove with the gun's silencer pressing against her ribs and knew that it was impossible at present to do anything but obey Andrew. Neither of them spoke and the silence, tactile in its intensity, was claustrophobic.

As they approached the Grand, Andrew said, 'Drive into the forecourt and park the car close against that wall. You can get out my side.'

Tara did as she was instructed and when she had switched off the engine, Andrew held out his hand.

'Keys,' he snapped and cramming them into his pocket opened the passenger door and got out. 'Now you, and remember even I can't miss at this range.'

Tara hoisted her legs over the gear

lever, slid across the passenger's seat and stood beside Andrew in the fresh air. She was only too aware of the muzzle of the gun against her as Andrew took her arm in a proprietorial manner and guided her across the forecourt, up the smooth marble steps and into the foyer of the hotel.

The Grand Hotel lived up to its name, its spacious entrance hall and reception area were luxuriously carpeted. Gracious arches gave on to an inner hall and a wide curving staircase. Flowers cascaded from pedestal vases and the whole was lit by a glittering chandelier whose pendant drops gleamed rather than sparkled, betraying the advance of the season. Even at this time of day there were plenty of people about. Several ladies took tea at the little tables beyond the reception, there was a waitress, prim in starched apron and cap and a receptionist at the desk.

Tara looked about her in the forlorn hope of aid, but the gun concealed under Andrew's raincoat still nudged her ribs and she allowed herself to be piloted to the lift without attracting anything more than a cursory glance from the waitress. The lift whisked them up to the third floor and emerging on to a deserted landing they approached the door of room 306.

Andrew jerked his head towards it and muttered, 'Try the door and no funny business.'

Tara turned the handle hoping it would be locked so that she would have to knock and thus at least give Simon some warning they were there, but in anticipation of her arrival Simon had left the door on the latch and it opened to her touch. In the moment of its opening Tara saw Simon, seated in an armchair, look up, smile in welcome.

She cried out to him, 'Simon! Look out!' But even as she warned, a violent push in the small of her back sent her spinning into the room, and Andrew stepped in after her, and pushed the door closed behind him with his foot.

'What the hell ... ?' exclaimed

Simon leaping to his feet as Tara sprawled in front of him.

'Shut up and sit down,' snarled Andrew, the raincoat tossed aside and the silenced gun in full view. Simon stared at Andrew and the pistol pointed unwaveringly at Tara and very slowly sank back into his chair.

'Better,' said Andrew. 'Stay there.' He prodded Tara with his foot. 'Get up, you.' Tara stumbled to her feet and groped for Simon. For a moment their hands touched, but Andrew barked, 'Get away from him,' and they jerked apart, both afraid of Andrew's nervous finger on the trigger. But even that brief contact had given mutual strength and steadied Tara's nerve; though still tensed to breaking point she felt less afraid, and she did as Andrew bid, moving away from the chair and turning bravely to face him.

'Get that tie,' he said nodding towards the tie lying on the bed, which Simon must have discarded while waiting for Tara to arrive.

'Tie his hands,' Andrew ordered, and as Tara hesitated with the tie twisting in her fingers, he pumped a bullet into the eiderdown beside her. The sound of the shot was no more than a muffled pop and she realised that should Andrew decide to shoot both of them, it would draw no more attention from outside the room than would a champagne cork.

Tara leapt away from the bed as the bullet buried itself not two feet from her and Simon said softly, 'Better do as he says, Tara. He's quite mad.'

'Mad am I?' grated Andrew. 'We'll see who's mad. Get on with it.' and while Tara knotted the tie round Simon's wrists, Andrew took a pair of cotton gloves from his pocket. Still covering his captives with the gun, he drew on the gloves.

'Take his belt off and do his ankles.'

With trembling hands Tara fumbled with Simon's buckle to remove his belt.

Andrew gave a mirthless laugh and said, 'Bet you wish she was taking that off for another reason, Hamilton.'

Tara siffened, but Simon looked calmly at Andrew over Tara's head as she knelt and tied the belt as loosely as she dared round Simon's legs.

'Your usual standard, Harper. You've a mind like a sewer.'

Andrew disregarded the remark and said, 'Back over here.'

Tara returned unwillingly to his side and he transferred the gun back to her ribs.

'Now, Hamilton, where's the envelope?'

'What envelope?'

'Another stupid answer like that will cripple your Tara.' Andrew's tone was clipped and low, and both Simon and Tara knew he meant what he said.

'Leave her alone,' shouted Simon. 'You can have your envelope. It won't help you though, my solicitor's seen it.'

'Too bad you won't be around to press charges,' drawled Andrew. 'They should never let murderers out of gaol. They are sure to kill again. A high percentage do, they say. Ironic really, isn't it? You'll be part of a statistic. First your wife and then in another 'crime passionel' you kill again, only this time your girlfriend succeeds in pulling the trigger of the gun in her death throes, and so, sadly, you kill each other.'

'You won't get away with it.'

'I? I was never here. There'll be no trace of me. There wasn't last time, was there?' Andrew's jeering had led him to an admission and Simon pounced on it.'

'So it was you who killed Jane.'

'I did the world a service as far as I can tell.'

'You'll go down for it,' said Simon.

'I doubt it. I might have if you hadn't so conveniently turned up that night. I'd decided to kill her anyway, she was a greedy little bitch and she pushed me too far. Then you came and had a blazing row with her and gave me the perfect opportunity.'

'Tobacco!' cried Simon. 'You smoke those revolting little cheroots. I smelled the tobacco in the flat. You were there then.'

Andrew nodded. 'Of course. She hustled me into the bedroom when you rang the bell, but my cigar was still smouldering in the ashtray. I had to remove it — er afterwards. I haven't made that mistake again though,' he went on indicating the heavy glass ashtray on the table by the door. 'See? Quite shining and unused. Now shall we get down to business? Where is that envelope?'

'But if you have the envelope why do you have to kill us?' cried Tara. 'You're safe once you've destroyed the photos.'

'Not really, you know about Jane and you know about the other envelopes. I'm intending to take over Jane's lucrative little business, you see. I could do with the extra cash, it'll help recoup my own losses. So,' he shrugged, 'I'm afraid you'll both have to go. Your solicitor as well, I think. Just to be on the safe side. I'll see Paul has a good upbringing. I'll love him like a father.'

The final gibe caused Simon to attempt to get up from the chair.

'Harper, so help me I'll — '

'Sit down!' roared Andrew and with one swift movement he kicked Simon back into the chair, then ripping off the chiffon scarf which caught Tara's hair at the nape of her neck, looped it lightly round her throat. Tara's hands flew to protect herself and she gasped for breath as with a twist and a jerk Andrew tightened the scarf and began to choke the life out of her.

Frantic now Simon cried, 'I'll tell you, I'll tell you where the photos are.'

'Too late, Hamilton. I'll bloody find them myself.' Andrew dropped the gun into his pocket and used both hands on the writhing Tara. As the scarf tightened inexorably round her neck, her vision blackened and the blood thundered in her ears; then she heard, as if from a great way off Simon bellow, 'Harper, look behind you.'

'Too old a trick to catch me,' panted Andrew and crumpled to the floor with a startled grunt as he was struck on the head by a heavy glass ashtray. Tara fell with him and the blackness which had threatened her overwhelmed her and she knew no more.

When she came to her senses again, she found herself lying on the bed with Simon leaning over her, his face grey with fear.

'Simon.' She tried to speak but discovered her voice was reluctant and made little sound.

'It's all right, darling, it's all all right. I'm here. The police and the doctor are on their way.' He stroked her hair back from her forehead and held her hand tightly in his own. As before, she felt a strange flow of strength at his touch and she managed to smile.

'Tell me,' she whispered. 'Tell me what happened. Where's Andrew?'

'Peter Alton, my solicitor remember, came up to meet you as I'd arranged with him. Harper closed the door but, thank God, he hadn't locked it. Remember I left the latch up for you?

And Peter, hearing me shouting as he reached the door, simply walked in. When he saw Harper strangling you, he just picked up the ashtray by the door and clouted him one with it.'

Peter Alton, who had been talking to the police on the telephone, replaced the receiver and turned to Tara.

'Are you all right?' he asked anxiously and when Tara nodded he smiled and said, 'Thank goodness. I was afraid I was too late.'

'Where's Andrew?' whispered Tara again, still unable to speak aloud.

'Over there,' said Simon grimly. 'Trussed up like a turkey. We've tied him to the chair so that he'll be no trouble when he comes round.'

The words brought sudden recollection to Tara and she sat up with a jerk.

'Paul!' she rasped. 'We must get to Paul.'

'Paul?' said Simon sharply. 'Where is he?'

'Old Court. Tied up. Bedroom.'

'Wait here. I'll be back.' Simon

started for the door and Tara, who despite the pain in her throat and neck was determined not to let him out of her sight again, struggled to get off the bed and go with him. He paused. 'Tara, you must stay here. The doctor's coming to see you. I'll be right back.'

'No.' Tara forced her voice to speak clearly. 'No.'

Simon recognised the determination in her eyes and held out his hand.

'Come on then. You hang on here, Peter. We'll be back. That bastard's got my son tied up at the guest house. We're going to fetch him.'

'But the police . . . ' began Peter.

'You deal with them. Tell them I'll be back; I need them just as much as they need me. Look after that,' he added, jerking his head in the direction of the still inert Andrew Harper.

'Will do. Don't be too long.'

As they crossed the elegant foyer and made for the car they collided with the police coming in.

'I'm afraid you can't leave now, sir,'

said a policeman firmly. 'We've report of an attempted murder.'

Hurriedly and with great force, Simon explained what had happened and once the policeman realised the situation he sent the rest of his men up to room 306 and escorted Tara and Simon to his police car.

'You won't mind if I accompany you, will you, sir? We'll take my car.'

We'll have to, thought Tara, remembering that Andrew had the keys to her car in his pocket, but she did not make the effort to speak, her throat was still too sore; she just clambered into the police car behind Simon, glad to be able to sit down again.

With the siren blaring they sped across town to Old Court, with Tara and Simon clinging to each other as the car swung round corners, tyres squealing and then screeched to a halt outside the guest house.

Simon leapt from the car and raced in at the front door, Tara hot on his heels. He took the two flights of stairs three at a time and came to a standstill outside the locked door. There was no key.

'Paul!' he called, his lips close to the key hole. 'Paul, are you all right?' And added after an imperceptible pause, 'It's me, Steven.'

A weak voice called in pathetic answer. 'Daddy. Please help me, Daddy.' On hearing Paul's appeal Simon seemed to grow in stature and as Tara and the policeman arrived puffing at the top of the stairs, he was preparing to break down the door.

'All right, Paul. Hold on, old son, we're coming in.'

It took their combined strength to force the door open and as it swung crazily on its damaged hinges, Simon was across the room and struggling with the knots which bound the child to the chair.

'Dad, oh, Daddy!' cried Paul and in the next moment he was safely in his father's arms.

Tara had paused in the doorway,

leaving Simon to find his son alone. The moment was too important to them both for them to share it. But even as the thought crystalized in her mind, Simon looked across at her over his son's head and holding Paul close to him with one arm, he held out the other to Tara.

LOVE'S DAWNING

Diney Delancey

Rosanne Charlton joins her friend Ruth and family for a holiday in Southern Ireland. Unfortunately, the holiday is marred for her by the arrival of Ruth's brother, Brendan O'Neill, whom Rosanne has always disliked. However, Brendan's presence is not Rosanne's only problem . . . Trouble and danger close round her, like an Irish mist, when she becomes unwittingly involved in mysterious activities in the bay — and finds herself fighting for survival in the dark waters of the Atlantic.

BETRAYAL OF INNOCENCE

Valerie Holmes

Annie works hard to keep her father from the poorhouse. However, she is wracked with guilt as she watches her friend, Georgette Davey, being used by Lady Constance. Annie longs to escape her life at the Hall, taking Georgette with her — but how? The arrival of the mysterious doctor, Samuel Speer, adds to her dilemma as Annie's concern for her friend grows. Georgette's innocence has been betrayed, but Annie is unaware of the threat that hangs over her own.

THE RELUCTANT BRIDE

Dorothy Purdy

Christine is forced into marriage with Adam Kyle, a wealthy and handsome entrepreneur whom she despises, in order to save her late father's reputation. At first Christine wants nothing to do with him; she tells him she hates everything he stands for. But during their honeymoon in the Friendly Islands her opinion of him changes, and she realises that she has misjudged him. Now she no longer feels embittered, true love blossoms among the sheltering palms.

SUSPICIOUS HEART

Joyce Johnson

Chantelle Wilde is a research interviewer for a film company, driving to Villefleurs in the South of France to interview the film star Heloise Remondin. But after she is hit by another car, the handsome driver, Phillipe Blanchard, insists on helping her to repair the damage. When she arrives at Madame Remondin's, she's surprised to discover that he is her grandson. Although she'd vowed never to love again, she hadn't reckoned with the arrogant Phillipe Blanchard.

DARK GUARDIAN

Rebecca King

When Fliss Naughton found herself stranded on a desert island with the mysterious Brand Carradine, she was at a loss as to what to do. He was her captor, but he was also her legal guardian — and she was at his mercy. Why then, as the time came for her to leave, did she find it increasingly difficult parting from him? Could it be that she truly longed for nothing better than to be by his side?